Festival of Time:
Book One:
Escape

Festival of Time: Book One: Escape

By C.L. Peache

Festival of Time: Book One: Escape

ISBN: 9798554236495

Independently published, available in paperback or e-book.

First published 2021

Cover design by Christine Goldschmidt

Typesetting by The Book Typesetters
thebooktypesetters.com
us@thebooktypesetters.com
07422 598 168

Acknowledgements

As always I find these difficult as so many people contribute to my books being published and I worry I will miss someone out... special thanks in no particular order...

Maria, Linda, Bonnie, Jane, Janice, Sophie, Alice, Karla, Ric, Tracey, Ste, Christine Goldschmidt for the stunning cover, Rachael and Nat at The Book Typesetters, and not forgetting, my Mum.

Part One

Chapter One – Luminosa – The Test

Thanan was awake early and keen to meet Pol and Star in the woods before their morning training started in the camp. The deep, dense forest of Luminosa provided the perfect place to practice without anyone seeing them, the belief in the Sucker's ability to block magic made the Masters complacent. If they got caught, the consequences didn't bear thinking about. Star had suffered at the hands of the Masters and had no desire to do so again.

Thanan often spent the first minutes wondering about the world he lived on. It was one of the daily tasks his trainer had suggested. "Think about your surroundings, Thanan. Question them. Learn from them. Think. Think. Think."

The children's magic wouldn't work in the camp. The 'Suckers' – as they called them – lived on the outskirts of the forest. From the talk in the camp, their magical powers blocked the use of magic everywhere other than the underground training rooms, where they were watched and monitored constantly. The punishment for disobedience was humiliation and pain.

They'd all heard the stories about the Suckers. No child had ever dared to venture to the outskirts to see if they were real; the Masters, with the help of some of the children, painted a terrifying picture of how they looked. In Thanan's nightmares he saw them as slugs the size of giant boulders, scattered around the camp, their antennae able to detect magic and suck it from the air. He wondered what they did with the magic. It made much more sense that they blocked magic rather than sucked it in, but Suckers sounded more sinister than

'Blockers'. It certainly scared the children into sticking to the rules... all except Thanan, Star and Pol. They needed to escape from Luminosa.

Thanan dropped quietly out of his hammock and onto the soft mossy floor. He could see Pol and Star were already waiting for him near the edge of the woods. It would be fully light in an hour and they needed to do the final test. The silver light of the morning would soon give way to the sapphire blue sky.

He nodded at the others as they made their way into the forest. He was annoyed when he noticed that Pol had decided to be a boy today. Thanan glared at them both but they averted their eyes. He hated it when Pol chose the boy, they were silly, and easily led by Star. He'd told Pol to come as a girl, as they were always more serious, and today was the most important of all the tests so far. He suspected Star had talked Pol into it. Thanan was distracted from his scowling thoughts when Star's small dragon flew over him, the tip of its small wing lightly skimming the top of his head as he dived for cover.

"Ha, ha," he said quietly, getting to his feet, "stop that, Star. Someone will see."

Star and Pol were sniggering, which made him angrier. Didn't they realise how serious this was? Star was always testing everyone's patience, but the moment she'd found out her magic creature was a dragon, she'd been more and more difficult to live with. She couldn't stop playing with it, much to the annoyance of everyone else. She had been warned repeatedly about her dragon swooping down on the other children, even though it was still a baby. More like an annoying large bat, Thanan liked to say when winding Star up; it looked menacing enough.

Strangely, the Suckers didn't work on the children who had magical creatures. They didn't know why. Not all the children were able to control creatures. With practice they could make the creatures invisible, which Star was putting all her energy into learning, as well as her aptly named, Dragon breathing fire.

"Oops, sorry, Thanan. Dragon got away from me. She does have a mind of her own, with her being the most dangerous and scary creature alive. How can I stop her?"

Thanan very much doubted that she wasn't able to stop her Dragon. Star had a natural ability and had been destined to have a magical creature, a bit like his ability to create spells. He glared at her once again and he could just see a hint of a blush.

He was extremely jealous of Star's creature. He didn't have the ability to control them, it had been his one wish that he could. His trainer told him that anyone could learn to control creatures – somehow, he very much doubted that. Thanan's skill lay in the ability to form complex magical spells. He could create them in his mind, layer upon layer until he released the spell. Eventually, he could probably magic up a dragon, a bigger dragon, which would swoop down on Star's. He smiled at the thought.

"Right, come on. Stop messing about. We haven't got loads of time."

"Okay, okay, whatever you say, Grand Master Thanan," Star said, the bravado back. She bowed low, her long legs stretching out behind her with her waist length blue hair falling in front of her face. When she straightened up and she looked at him, her bright blue eyes were twinkling with mischief.

Pol sniggered again, and Thanan glared at them. They looked abashed. He couldn't be mad at Pol for long though, not when they looked all of five-years-old. No-one knew how old Pol was. The Masters didn't know Pol's age, and no-one knew where they came from since they weren't allowed to talk about it. Sometimes the new children would talk about their home worlds as if they could remember them; but they were soon warned against it.

Pol was wearing their usual dungarees and long feathery boots. Pol never changed their clothes whether they were a boy or a girl, the only difference was to the colour of their eyes; they were bright purple when a boy, and bright orange when a girl, and Pol's demeanour was subtly different. They were very minor changes, and not everyone could tell – although their attitude was probably the biggest change if you knew them well enough. Pol's blonde cropped hair made them look pixie like although no-one knew what a pixie looked like but they had overheard one of the Masters comment on Pol more than once. Thanan was thinking again, Tobias would be proud.

His friends finally under control, they moved deeper into the forest. There was an abundance of multi-coloured bell-shaped flower-heads all seemingly asleep under the silver sky. As Pol walked through the clearing, they raised their arms, and the flowers started to hum. Gently, the flower heads moved towards the sky; like sunflowers seeking out the sun. The silver light danced over the tops, and the noise grew louder; it was as if the flowers were singing to the light of the breaking dawn.

Pol smiled, until they saw Thanan's face, then they quickly lowered their hands, and the sound abruptly stopped. Pol could not only gender-shift between male and female, but they also had a natural ability to communicate with their surroundings. Pol was tiny, but their presence thrummed large with magic. Sometimes out of the corner of Thanan's eye he thought he saw a giant; but when he focused – they were back to their normal size. Pol would have a gleam of knowing in their eyes, as if this five-year-old was a thousand years old.

Making their way carefully, and now quietly, they moved deeper into the thick forest where they wouldn't be seen. Above them, the silver sky was blocked out by the lantern trees. The massive trunks and thick branches needed to support the weight of the heavy lantern-shaped flower-heads. During the day they hung down towards the flowery carpeted floor, during the night they pointed to the sky – emitting a soft glow. The three of them had decided to test Pol's abilities further by harvesting some of the light inside them and using it to see in the dark, like their own personal nightlights. They'd tried to think of all the items they might need once they'd escaped Luminosa.

Star naturally fell into step with Thanan, as Pol continued ahead, gently touching the flowers but making sure they didn't make a noise. Pol looked happiest when they were amongst nature.

"Do you think we're ready, Thanan?" Star asked.

He answered more confidently than he felt, "Yes."

But were they ready? Did they know what they were doing? Would it work? They needed to leave Luminosa; Star would be taken soon, and Thanan would follow a few days later. Star would be turning thirteen soon and that's when the children left and no-one knew where they went, because no-one ever came back to tell. They had to get out together. They wouldn't let anyone split them up. Tobias had helped him find a way; Thanan just hoped it would work.

Star broke up his thoughts, "I cannot imagine not being with you and Pol forever. Being split up would be the worst thing that has ever happened to me."

Thanan was touched by Star's words. She was normally the fearless, jokey girl. Always quick to anger and defend her friends, but the first one to laugh. A twinkle of mischief was never far from her eyes. It made Thanan realise how close they were to leaving, and how dangerous it was.

Pol appeared in the middle of them. Their small feet made no impression on the soft mossy floor. Pol took each of their hands and smiled at them in turn, and then started running.

Laughing quietly with delight, the sadness of the moment broken, the friends raced through the forest, grateful for this time together.

"Okay, I think that's far enough," Thanan said. By now they were deep into the lantern trees, and the little clearing provided the perfect area. They didn't want to venture too far; the stories of the monsters at the borders not something any of them wished to discover were true.

"Right then Pol, do your thing," Star said.

Pol smiled, closing their eyes and shimmered in and out of focus.

"Okay, Thanan, try now," Star said, not able to hide the excitement from her voice.

Thanan muttered the words for the levitation spell and he started to rise towards the treetops. Star clapped her hands in delight and started to lift off the ground. It didn't take long before they were at the top of one of the giant trees. It was amazing. Looking down, Thanan felt a little dizzy, Pol was a small dot on the ground. Reaching inside his cloth bag, he retrieved the glass phial and placing it carefully inside the flower, he tipped it slightly and filled it with the lantern sap which they could use to light the dark nights once they'd escaped. Star was doing the same. Once full, he put it in his pocket and perched on a branch which was thicker than his body and looked out across their world.

For two hours after midnight the sky remained golden, and then turned silver. After that, every four hours the sky changed to a different colour. The sapphire blue was now signalling the morning, they had better leave soon. Thanan's stomach lurched, but it was more about the thought of their plans to leave this world than the height. This place was the only home they knew; well, the only one he remembered. Not that he liked to think of it as home. What would the other worlds be like? Surely it had to be better than this one? At least they now knew that Pol could stop the Suckers' ability to block their magic. Secretly they'd tried over months and months, and the range seemed unlimited. They had tried it with other children, but it only worked with him and Star. They couldn't figure out why.

Thanan slipped off the branch to make his way back down, and immediately realised something was wrong. He just managed to hold onto the nearest branch. His body felt heavy. He could no longer use his magic. The faint laughter in his mind told him that Pol had switched off their power; he could no longer levitate! His legs dangled in fresh air.

'Ha, ha, ha, stop messing about. When I get down, you'd better be a girl again, Pol. You two are just childish," he said,

using the telepathic bond they had to berate them. He didn't want to shout out loud and alert anyone nearby. Another gift they shared, and the only way they could communicate with Pol as they didn't speak.

He could feel the magic coursing through him again and gently lowered himself down. Pol had turned into a girl and was taking this whole situation more seriously, finally. Star was grinning, as usual. He had never met another child as happy as Star. Nothing made her sad; well, other than the thought of them being split up.

When he landed on the soft mossy floor, he checked his phial; all still in one piece. They would have to be careful to keep them hidden from the Masters and the other children. They wrapped them in some large leaves from the tree; careful to use the ones that had been discarded. Pol wouldn't let anyone harm anything in the forest. The light worked only when their hand touched the phial, so the leaf would keep it hidden and safe.

Thanan had managed to hide them just in time for lessons to start. He parted from his friends: Star off to train with Dragon, and Pol to do whatever they did. As he lined up ready to go into the cave, he spotted that Triana was first in line, as usual. On his first day in the training rooms she'd pushed everyone out of the way so she could pick the best trainer. It hadn't worked out the way she had planned, and they had been enemies ever since.

Chapter Two – Arcus – The Quest

He stormed out of the throne room, seething. Villian was so angry, he could still hear the laughter from the room as he stalked down the corridor, his leather boots loud on the stone slabs. He felt the loss of his sword; no weapons were allowed in the council chambers. He pushed through the ornate doors, not waiting for the guards to open them.

It was a good idea; he knew it was. It was the only answer, but he couldn't make them see it. Who was he after all? Prince Villian, eventually to become the King of Arcus, it mattered not one bit. They all saw him as a child. He was seventeen now, nearly eighteen and he had come of age. The adults didn't know what to do, so why didn't they listen to him? What did they know? All superior in their past knowledge and experience, and deaf to brave and heroic deeds.

Their world was failing and they needed help. The commoners knew something was afoot, but not the extent of the danger their very way of life was facing. The grip his family had on Arcus was fragile. Soon the realm would fall, and they needed the dragons to return, but they hadn't been seen for thousands of years. People no longer believed they were real, despite a library that told their story; a children's tale was their answer. His anger was fuelled by their ignorance. During the Festival of Time, some of the true believers would offer up gifts in the hope they would come back, but as the years passed they expected their prayers and offerings to go unanswered. Why did they still bother if they didn't believe? Fools.

Villian powered his long, muscly legs faster and faster, until he broke into a run; through the castle, up the stairs, nearly knocking over a poor maid on the way. He shouted an apology as he climbed, his legs burning, his lungs on fire. He shot out onto the battlements and sped around the walls hoping to burn away his anger. Nowhere did he feel the power of the kingdom and the weight of responsibility, the determination to succeed, than on the top of the dominating castle, his home.

Finally, he stopped to survey his land, breathing hard but feeling the anger diminishing and his resolve hardening. The thriving markets below were buzzing with life. More and more people had been arriving in the city, and they were busier than ever – that added further challenge, as more people brought more problems and thieves. There was fear of the imminent battle to come. He could feel it in the air; if others could not, or would not, acknowledge it. The markets gave way to a bustling harbour, the war fleet anchored offshore to enable the fishing boats free access to the docks. When the wind turned, the smell of the harbour tickled his nose, the fishy smell a permanent aroma on the people who lived there.

Past the fishing harbour lay the port where the war fleet normally docked, the sailors making the most of their shore time. The fleet had moved offshore to allow for his project. His belly felt the excitement of his plans soon to come to fruition. He would show them what life would be like under Prince Villian's rule. His father's plans would seem childish in comparison. His plans were for future generations, not just to settle old debts and pander to rich merchants. He'd already decided what kind of king he would be. He'd been taught well, despite having his father as a role model.

"Fancy a fight?"

The voice of his sword trainer; forever challenging.

"I could beat you even out of breath. You've got old, Master Sword."

Villian turned to see a flash of silver pass his face. He ducked at the last moment and felt the air whistle near his ear.

Some of the soldiers gathered to watch. One of them threw their prince his sword, honoured to have it touched by him.

Villian grinned at the sword master. He held the sword with a practised callused hand, ready to fight.

They fought for what felt like hours, Villian pushing his anger to the back of his mind and focusing on beating his adversary. Emotion held no place in combat. Finally, they decided to call it a draw, both sweating and happy.

He embraced Morbark. His teacher asked, "Have you calmed down now, my Prince?"

Villian nodded. The laughter of the council had passed, but he held it inside for when he needed the anger, and he knew he would. Wiping the blade, he handed it back to the soldier; maybe the fact that his prince had held his sword would make him stand strong when the time came. The Gods knew they would need to have nerves of steel. Villian's prowess with a sword was well known, but to see two of the best swordsmen in Arcus battle, would be a tale to be told later around a fire. The soldiers didn't know a fighter was capable of such moves. Such stories were how a kingdom was held together. Their actions were just as important as the stories. Not many had seen Villian's warriors train. They were a sight to behold and he knew they could help turn the tide of a battle.

As they made their way off the battlements, Morbark said, "Tell me what has made you so angry, my Prince."

"The council; always the council. They know nothing, Master Sword. If they and my father have their way, we will all be killed. The army is coming. This betrothal between the two houses is a waste of our time – a sham. It's for the people they say. Another lie. The power of our Kingdoms will not save us from the slaughter. I don't know how many times I need to tell them. We need to think bigger."

Morbark put his hand on his arm, a testament to their friendship that he felt he could touch his prince so informally. Villian lowered his voice, not wanting the soldiers or other keen ears to hear. This wasn't their worry, they had to focus on their job, and he knew people whispered to Baynard, which would be passed straight to his father.

"It's difficult for them, Prince Villian, after thousands of years they don't want to believe. With belief comes hope. With hope, comes disappointment. You of all people must understand. I've never known someone so skilled with the sword as well as the pen. A faster learner, barely anyone bothered with the library before you were born. Well, maybe your mother loved it as much. You are loved by all; that is rare in a ruler and it can welcome jealousy. You must be careful."

Villian listened to these wise words. His mother had been the driving force behind him before her death. He gave thanks every day that she created who he was today. Left with only his father's teachings, he knew it would have been different. She had believed in the old stories.

At night she had told him the stories of humans and dragons keeping peace on their worlds for countless generations. The power of the dragons was never challenged. The potential of their fury too devastating. The history books told an unbelievable story. Dragons became allergic to humans; or so the stories told. For such a thing to happen! The healers couldn't help. Nothing helped. A war had started with those who became known as the Masters. Eventually the dragons had to leave, taking their magic and protection with them, but beating the threat of the Masters before they left, or so they had thought. Many accounts said that this had been caused by magic. Unrest had followed the dragons' departure, and now, finally, thousands of years later, they were losing. They needed the dragons to return; it was their only hope.

Scouring the history books, Villian had read about magic. He often spoke the word out loud. Magic. What a word: it conjured up so many images, especially to someone who devoured the old stories. Villian had only spoken to one person about his discovery. He couldn't talk to anyone in the castle; they were closed off to such things and no-one of importance believed in dragons anymore. "Where are these protectors of our world?" Why haven't they come to save us if they are real?" they would cry, dismissing it as a child's fantasy.

Because you don't believe, was all Villian could think, and you're too scared to do anything about it.

"Thinking again? All the time you're thinking. You have your mother in you that's for sure."

Villian smiled at Morbark. His mother was constantly with him, driving his beliefs and decisions. They stopped before the stairs leading into the castle, and Villian looked again over the lands that would be his if they survived.

The flat plains gave way to stunning mountain ranges, topped with snow in the distance. The great forests dominated a lush, green hunting ground where stags bellowed their warnings during the mating season. But past that, the lands hid the army they knew would fall on the castle. It was just a matter of time.

He imagined what his father would say if he knew what he was doing. No-one went to see Raykan, the outcast. Children told scary night-time stories about him, and girls swooned with fear if they saw him, although it was a rarity for him to leave his home deep in the woods anymore.

Villian would admit the old man was hideous to look at. He'd been burnt badly, and it almost looked like he had dragon scales covering his face. It was why Villian had sought him out, and he had not been disappointed. Raykan had more knowledge than anyone in the castle about the history of Arcus. He'd agreed to help Villian if he, in turn, borrowed books from the great castle library. Somewhere Raykan could not access. It was an advantageous deal on both parts.

Reaching the ground level, he said goodbye to the Master Sword and made his way through the secret passages and out of the protection of the castle to Raykan's hut. He'd needed to change out of his princely attire. Being seen in his finery, wouldn't help him to move through the shadows. He changed into commoner's clothes and covered himself with a hood to avoid being recognised. Not an easy task for someone everyone knew. Especially from the girls. He sighed, thinking about the upcoming wedding. A union with another family would make them stronger his father said. He was wrong. Villian didn't want to marry; he was a soldier, a warrior, a protector of Arcus. He wasn't looking forward to this union. But he would do his duty.

The dusty stone door had closed behind him. Hood up, Villian made his way through the castle streets. The atmosphere had changed over the last few months. The castle had kept the secrets about the oncoming army, but the people could feel the change. The place felt subdued, with the underlying fear in the air he'd detected on the battlements. On the street he could nearly taste it.

The stone pathway gave way to the grass. Villian took a deep breath, he much preferred the outdoors to the stuffy castle walls. He felt jealous of the birds, so free to fly where they wanted, while he forever had the heavy chains of duty to hold him fast to the ground. He imagined being a dragon, riding a dragon. Villian had dreamed of dragons before he'd even known what they were. Most children don't remember their dreams, but he always had. No-one in the castle believed him of course, so he stopped mentioning the vivid dreams he'd had from a baby. Only Raykan believed him. He knew the real truth.

They didn't have long until the world would be forever changed. It was up to them to change the tide against the oncoming army. They needed the dragons, and they needed them now. Villian would set forth like the princes of old. He would go forth on the biggest adventure ever told. He would bring back the dragons.

Chapter Three – Suntra – The Dragons

Pathanclaw stretched his immense wings. It felt good to wake, but he knew this would be his last chance. If he failed to leave Suntra when the Festival of Time opened and find a way to bring his family through later, his species, which had ruled for endless time with the humans, would never leave this planet. Never return to Arcus. Even their mighty magic had been no match, their powers drawn from the power of the gems which the humans had greedily used for their own selfish purposes, making them all weaker. It had made it impossible to stay on Arcus. He'd hoped the humans had learned their lesson; they should never have been given the secrets of Magic.

He wondered, as he had many times before, if it would be so bad to stay here. They had a fortunate life. But he felt the pull, a need within him. There was another of their kind that needed his help; they were hidden from him now, but experience told him to be patient. If they stayed, the dragons would die out forever. They had to leave Suntra, and soon. Pathanclaw knew they only had one more chance. Time was changing, his old bones felt the change, like a human felt the change of a season.

He shook his giant head wondering how he knew this. Before he left Suntra, he needed to prepare the rest of his family. Their innocent years had come to an end. It was time for them to decide to stay here in peace, or to go forth and help the humans once again; not that he felt they had much choice. No females had been born on Suntra since they'd arrived on this planet. They had lost many dragons, including most of their adult females when they had fled Arcus.

His red scales glinted in the gem encrusted cave. Only royal dragons were born with red scales. The humans placed everything below their precious gold, but red was the fire of dragons. The arguments he'd had with them. But the shine of the gold won over a human heart every time. He didn't mind; all gems were a dragon's friend; their magic was stronger using the power of the precious stones. To dragons it was nectar, as was ale to a human.

The rest of the great families had chosen a mating pair to send to this world, as well as other key dragons to help the survival of their species. Their lineage needed to continue; all except the great purple dragons who had been lost to time. Pathanclaw had been forced to make the choice for his family all those years ago. Who was to stay and die; who was to leave and possibly survive? He wished he could have stayed; but he was the head of the great families and his sacrifice had not been allowed. For that he would be eternally grateful, guilty, and resentful, as it came with great sadness at leaving his kin behind, especially when he felt responsible. He had of course accepted; his wife was pregnant with their son at the time, the next heir.

They had survived their flight and made it to Suntra, and the families had thrived under his leadership. It had been hard at times; they did not bear children quickly. He'd had to be hard. Dragons were by nature stubborn creatures until they came of age. They could be more than a handful as the humans would say. More than a few of the nannies ended up with singed wings when the children decided to play up. His deep chuckle woke his wife.

"What has amused you today?" Her thought came into his mind.

"Just thinking of the children. Do you know Pathandon couldn't stop breathing fire the other day and the nannies had to clip his wings and drop him in the lake?"

He felt her responding chuckle, *"You favour him. The others will know it."*

"I know. He reminds me so much of myself. Headstrong and a know-it-all. Brave and..."

"Stupid... Yes, he takes after his grandfather in many ways."

Silvarna stretched, as he had. They had long since stopped having children. But their grand-dragons were a joy to behold. Even though Pathandon was the last of their lineage, they considered all the other dragons kin.

As King and Queen of the Kingdom they looked out with joy at what they had created. Kings and Queens were names from the humans, as were children and many other words they had adopted over time. They didn't have words for such things but it amused them to use some of the old names. It might also make it easier if they were ever joined again, on this world or their home world of Arcus.

Dragon history was told through stories: they knew their lineage and great deeds and failures of their family history. Only the king knew all the tales. Pathanclaw had adopted the humans' love of storytelling as well as their customs. He didn't like being called a king, but he couldn't change it now, even if he wanted to.

Each morning and night they would all gather, and stories would be told. Tales of great battles of the past: both young and old needed to learn from past mistakes. If Pathanclaw's plan worked, they would all soon be returning to Arcus and there would be death. Were the lives of his friends, his family worth it? Maybe not, but the bond with the humans was too strong and they needed help. The time had finally come, he felt it. The one had been born. They also needed to find the lost female dragons. If they still survived. Somehow, they had to live on.

From these stories he hoped that they could learn how to defend the world so they could live in peace once more. The Masters had been defeated as they left, the same as the dragons, but doubt was a constant at the back of his mind. He felt them lurking in the darkness, plotting their return. They were forever greedy for the magic that gave them so much power. The shift in Pathanclaw was testament that they were planning another attack, that they had survived. The Festival of Time was opening a window for more than just his kind to move; dangerous times were ahead.

Pathanclaw looked across the expanse of their temporary home. He felt a swell of pride at the sight. Would it be enough? Could his family return and save the humans? Would the female dragons be found? His memories lived more and more in the past but he was trying to learn. What did they need to do to stop the Masters once and for all? How could he change the mistakes of the past? Could the prophecy be true? They had to try, before Arcus and his friends were destroyed forever.

He silenced the group now gathered with one thought as he moved to the entrance of his home. The younglings were as rowdy as ever, but they immediately quietened at his command; even his grandson, which was a miracle and wouldn't last long. As always, Pathandon was settled near Bluewing; best friends, as he was with Bluewing's father. Today they would tell the stories of their friendships with the humans. Only a few of the elders had communicated with humans. Six of the seven great families had sent kin through successfully. Luckily, they had sired children, but no females had been born. Most had only known this world. The dragons needed to see the humans as their equal, be able to live amongst them and protect them as they had for thousands of years.

His thoughts returned to the past as his wife Silvana started the story, mindful of his distracted thoughts.

The glorious days in the throne room, the celebrations and coronations of kings and queens. The sadness of friends passing. He envied and pitied the humans' short lifespan. They, of course, knew loss and grief in their short time, often more keenly than dragons. Human emotions were unpredictable at best. Teaching them how to use magic was, without doubt, the worst decision that had ever been made. Sadly they had discovered some humans also needed saving from themselves. The greed for power had resulted in the ultimate betrayal. Pathanclaw missed his friends. He hoped that they still lived as they would need their knowledge and power in the coming struggle.

'Pay attention my dear.' Silvarna had passed the story telling onto one of the younger dragons. They in turn would learn and teach, thus passing the legends through the generations. Although they had a king and queen, they preferred everyone to be on equal terms where tradition and the natural order of things allowed. No one should be more or less than another, but some needed more guidance than others.

'Sorry, my dear. My age is finally catching up with me. I find myself living in the past. I wonder what the future will bring. If we are successful and once again live in peace with the humans as was meant to be and is foretold, will it be the same?'

'I very much doubt it will be the same, my love. But different is not always bad. Future generations will have their own ideas about their lives and how they want to live them. The important point to remember is that they get to live them. Really live them, like we have here.'

Pathanclaw looked at his Queen. She was beautiful. A full red dragon, although as with himself, she had flashes of age now, and she complained as did he when the wings didn't unfold as quickly as they used to. She moved closer and nuzzled him, before adding, *'In your heart you know it will not be the same for us. We have seen so much, and it is nearing the time that our lives become a story to be told to future generations. We do this for them, so that they can build a new future. It might not be like ours, but it will be peaceful, and they will be happy. That is our role in this story. This is what we will make come true.'*

'You're so wise my love. I hope we have a little more time for peace, and I would like to see old friends before the end.'

'Well, my love, we are still alive now, so let's enjoy the time with our family, and the precious moments we have left before

you leave. Come listen to Bluewing tell the story, he keeps getting the names mixed up and no-one wants to correct him. It's his first time at the storytelling. Maybe you could have a little word afterwards and set him on the right path.'

Pathanclaw tuned into the thoughts of Bluewing and chuckled. He was indeed mixing up the story. Dining on humans was not something that was or would be encouraged in the future. He could feel the mirth of the others, but it wasn't their way to humiliate. He would have a quiet word with Bluewing so he would know for next time. He looked at his grandson and he was surprised he had not made some comment to his friend; maybe he was growing up and learning how to manage others. It was an encouraging sight.

Chapter Four – Luminosa

There was no certain time or age when they were taken to the cave. Some children were there years and some only days before they were tested. Thanan had been so nervous when his time came. There had been five new children, including the one who would become his arch nemesis, Triana. She had confidently stridden forward, making sure she was first in line for everything. They'd been led out of camp by a Master and as they left the warmth of the forest, they entered the cool of the cave. The sound of rushing water was overwhelming, and Thanan struggled to hear the instructions from the Master over the noise. They were pushed further and further into the cave.

One of the children started crying and was soon quietened with a word from the Master. Thanan didn't dare look behind him. He used all his concentration to stop himself from slipping and falling into the icy water flowing past. The Master held up phials of light to show the way. They turned a corner and in front of them was a waterfall so high they couldn't see the top. The water cascaded past him and deep into the cave, a fine mist settling on his hair and clothes.

They were led to the side of the waterfall where Thanan could make out a boat. His eyes met Triana's and he could see a flicker of fear cross her face before she faked confidence and laid on her back in the boat, as instructed. There were ropes tied to both ends and someone on the other end started pulling the boat through the dark, bleak, tunnel ahead; but to where?

When it came to Thanan's turn, he wasn't sure if he would be able to do it. He was feeling cold and miserable and the thought of going into an even darker, colder part of the cave didn't appeal. But what choice did he have? He lay on the boat and closed his eyes, the slats at the bottom digging into his back. As the boat started moving, he tentatively opened one eye.

"Wow."

"SHHH," came the harsh reply.

Thanan put his hand over his mouth. He opened both eyes and stared at the sight above him. Millions and millions of lights were hanging off the roof. They dangled like a chain of water droplets. What he thought would be a dark passageway was stunningly beautiful. He would come to learn from Tobias that these were called glow worms, and they only lived a few short weeks.

Moments later he made it through the narrow underground river, and nothing could have prepared him for the sight in the cave. His mouth dropped open as one of the Masters pulled him roughly from the boat and pushed him over to where the other children were equally open-mouthed in the centre of the cave.

"I've never seen anything like it," exclaimed one boy. This earned him a piercing look from one of the Masters. They looked menacing enough with their long black hooded capes; they didn't need to add a look or word to scare the children. One of Masters explained that this was their new training room and that a trainer would choose them, depending on their magical ability. One of the boys whispered that the green worms were supposed to do bad magic. Thanan nudged him to be quiet.

Massive worms hung from the ceiling of the giant opening in the cave. The glow from them mirrored the colours of their world: gold, silver, sapphire blue, emerald, ruby, purple and pitch-black onyx. Thanan was sure the girl Triana would get the green one.

"Form a line."

The one called Triana pushed her way to the front. She was probably barely five years old, the same age as Pol looked now, but she had an attitude that surpassed any other.

She had been called forward and pointed to a green worm near the top of the cave. She'd looked smugly at Thanan, her mean, brown eyes challenging him. She flicked back a strand of her long, curly brown hair and walked towards the centre of the cave.

Later he would come to learn about all the different colours of their world. The emerald green was considered the best for learning magical spells, but also like the boy had said, they were considered to be 'bad' or 'dark' magic. The purple tanzanite ones were considered the highest level of learning, but no-one knew when the last child had been chosen by this worm for teaching.

Thanan had waited nervously. The two Masters kept looking at him and whispering. After much discussion he was called over and told to stand in the middle of the room and lie low in a floating hammock, like the ones they slept in. It was hanging menacingly in the middle of the cave. He lay in the chair as instructed and when it started to float, he was terrified. It felt like he was going to fall off any minute, but afterwards he thought it had been pretty amazing. His hammock moved upwards, past a glaring Triana and her green worm, and right to the top of the cave. He had been chosen by the tanzanite worm, much to the surprise of everyone, judging by some of the gasps he heard below and the strange looks the Masters gave him when he returned the cave floor hours later.

The cave became his favourite place in the camp. He could feel the power of magic course through his body as he relaxed, waiting for the joining of their minds. In the heart of their world, the magic was strong. The light emitted from the glow worms was like millions of stars shining down, and the large glow worms were like planets in the solar system Tobias had told him about. The worm would be their guide, mentor and teacher while they were there. But they only ever spoke to children. He'd never seen a Master with them, in fact they rarely saw any Masters in the camp. However if anything displeased them, they soon appeared. Thanan named his worm Tobias; he would become his best friend. When Thanan was laying in the hammock just below Tobias, the worm would hover just above his head, and the transfer of minds would begin.

After morning training Thanan headed outside to find his friends. The green sky had passed to red and next would be his favourite purple colour. Star said it was because he was obsessed with Tobias and that the worm was his favourite.

He found Star and Pol sitting in the clearing enjoying their late breakfast. Thanan chose a food ball off one of the bushes and went to join them, stretching out on the short mossy grass.

"Good morning," Thanan said.

"Morning," said Star, "fancy seeing you for the first time today."

Thanan rolled his eyes, she couldn't be more obvious if she tried.

"Yes, so lovely to see you as always Star." He couldn't hide the sarcasm from his voice which is just what she wanted, and she grinned at him, her mouth full of food. She squished it through her teeth and smiled at him.

"That's disgusting, Star."

Closing her mouth, she chewed and swallowed before opening her mouth and sticking out her tongue. "All gone. Can I have some more?"

Quick as a flash Thanan leapt over and grabbed her arms trying to pin them to the ground. She laughed delightedly and fought back. This was nearly a daily occurrence for the pair.

"Oh, look. The young lovers making out on the grass. How romantic."

Thanan groaned, getting off his friend. Star raised herself onto her elbows and eyed Triana. She hadn't changed in the last five years, in fact, she had gotten worse. Thanan positioned himself so he could grab her arms if she tried anything. They didn't need any trouble and specifically Star being locked up again for attacking Triana, however, justified.

"For your information, Triana, Thanan and I are simply best friends. Unfortunately, you wouldn't understand as you don't have any actual friends."

"Don't I? What are these then?" Triana gestured at the five children standing behind her.

"Oh, that's easy. They are what I would call victims, prisoners. I could go on, but MY friends and I, have more important things to do."

Triana scoffed. "Like what exactly? Hang about with your weirdo friend Pol. The freak." Before Star could launch herself, Triana and her hangers-on moved away.

"Stupid child. One day I'm going to set Dragon on her and make her burn those long, curly locks right off her head."

Dragon tried to create fire and a small puff of smoke emerged. Star laughed and clapped her hands in delight, "Well done my fabulous Dragon. You keep trying and one day we will burn her to a crisp."

"Star, don't be mean. I don't like her either, but we all have different ways of coping."

"Dragon rot! That one is evil, plain and simple."

There was no point arguing since they'd had this conversation many times before. Throughout this whole interaction Pol had sat cross-legged behind Thanan, avoiding everyone's eye.

'Anyway, I talked to Tobias about our plans and he thinks we have everything ready now. He said we just need to hold tight.'

Thanan preferred to talk via minds when they were in a group, then to the outside, they appeared to be three friends sitting quietly, eating food together.

'Are you ready for this, Thanan? I'm so excited. The Festival of Time is in two weeks! We are going to get away from this horrible place. Free to explore time and worlds, getting away from hateful people. I think I might explode with excitement.'

'Before you explode, we need to make sure we have everything in place. Keep calm, and act normal. We don't want anyone guessing why you're so excited and finding out what we are doing!'

'Okay, I'm not completely stupid you know. Right, I'm having a nap before training. I'm tired after getting up early.'

'Sounds like a good idea.' Thanan lay back and closed his eyes.

Tobias had told him that the Festival of Time only happened once every thousand years. Portals would open across worlds for a year, and it would be their chance to escape. After hesitating, Tobias had told him that others had tried in the past and failed. But they hadn't had him to help and guide them and he knew that Thanan and his friends would make it.

Thanan had been studying other worlds whenever he could, as they needed to know which world they were aiming for. There was no point ending up somewhere that was worse than theirs. As long as they stayed together, though, it didn't really matter. They didn't know what they were going to do when they got there – but they could figure that out; or he hoped they could. He had a feeling that Tobias knew more than he was communicating. Thanan had no doubt the Masters would come after them. Then what would they do? They didn't know enough magic yet to fight the power of the Masters. Even with Pol's strange powers, although Thanan wasn't sure Pol could use it against people.

"Daydreaming again, Thanan? You need to live in the moment you know."

He opened his eyes and looked at a smiling Star, he wasn't going to take the bait.

"How long have I been asleep?"

"About an hour. It's time for us to go back."

Thanan stretched, wondering where the time had gone. He took another bite of his food, enjoying the luscious flavours. The sky would soon be changing to purple, which meant it was time for lessons.

Saying goodbye, he made his way to grab some more food before going to the cave. He was hungry after going into the forest early this morning. He never failed to be amazed by the food bushes. He had absorbed so much from Tobias about other worlds; some had to grow and make food, which was totally weird. In his world you picked a food ball off one of the bushes, something that Tobias said was the size of an apple, and it gave you all the nutrients you needed. Tobias talked about flavour, but all the food tasted the same from the food bushes. Amazing but he couldn't tell Tobias what that flavour was. Triana had developed a spell that changed it to the worst taste ever. Some of the Sucker's out there didn't like them, as her magic shouldn't have been able to work in the camp, but she was one of the Masters favourites, so Thanan guessed she was given special privileges.

Finally, he was full up and he made his way back to the cave. He was sad that it was his final weeks with Tobias, but they had to leave before Star turned thirteen and was taken – two days after the Festival of Time.

Chapter Five - Arcus

Weeks later Villian was covered in dust and couldn't stop sneezing. He was glad he'd tied his hair back. His long black hair would be streaked with silver just like his fathers, but at least his would wash out. His dark hair was one of the few things he'd inherited from his father along with his darker skin. His mother had been as white as the alabaster stone they mined. The stone statues in the Kings Hall were a shocking likeness of her.

Despite the dust, he loved being in the library. His father had no use for them, and it was only because everyone feared the Keeper of Books, that it hadn't been torn down and the books used to fuel the fires in the castle.

When Raykan had first suggested that he would only help him if he 'borrowed' the books, Villian nearly gave up there and then. The Keeper of Books was terrifying – even though his words were as rare as the compliments from his father. One look above his glasses was statement enough.

Over the years he'd had hundreds, or what felt like millions of hours of lessons with the Keeper. Even though his father held no value in books, his mother had, and surprisingly his father had allowed this to continue after his mother had died. But he'd still never spoken more than a handful of words to the Keeper. Villian would turn up to his lesson, a book would be laid out on the table with instructions of which passages to read and then he would have to answer pre-written questions about the passage. This was the part Villian hated. He was a master swordsman, a lover of sailing, and devoured knowledge from reading every book he could, but he despised writing.

Even though he'd mastered it, it didn't stop him hating it, but a great king needed to master more than just the sword.

He smiled at his innocence and rubbed his hand in memory. In the early days, he'd taken the questions and paid one of the servants to write the answers as he dictated them. When he had returned the next day there was no book on the table only a quill and parchment. The words read...

Write this passage until I tell you to stop...

I, Prince Villian, will never cheat again, and from this day until the end of time, all the work I produce will be my own.

His hand had ached for weeks after. His fingers were so cramped he'd had to miss sword training for the next week. Never again had he ever asked anyone to do his work. That was one of the words the Keeper of Books had spoken, "Stop." Just that, nothing else. He felt like he'd been writing for days and there had been no break for food or comfort.

"Ah ha." Villian spoke louder than he meant, and daren't turn around to check if the Keeper had noticed. He knew he would have heard, the man had hearing better than any bat. He tutted if anyone turned a page loudly.

Villian could barely breathe. He ran his hand along the large volume. This was the book Raykan had sent him to search for. During all the years he'd dedicated any spare time he had to searching for this precious item. Not that a prince had much spare time; there was always some duty to perform. It was the book; of that he was certain. He'd never seen anything like it before.

Folding his legs in front of him, he laid the large book over his lap. The cover was aged and running his hands over it, it felt like thick tough leather and the front felt like dragon scales. Could he be touching a dragon? There were two metal clasps in the shape of dragon claws that held the spine. He was familiar with most metals, having been interested in sword making and pestering the smithy daily until he told him everything. He made a mental note to ask the smithy about the clasps.

The clasp was stranger still. S shaped metal was interwoven down the front, holding the pages secure. The colours drew his breath into a whistle. They bled into one another: silver, gold, blue, green, red, purple and black. He didn't think he'd ever seen anything so beautiful, and his father had amassed treasure from all corners of the lands, getting the best jewellers to make him bigger and better objects which adorned the castle.

"Wow." The word escaped him before he could stop himself. He tensed, waiting for the inevitable tut that would follow his abuse of the silence. He heard a shuffle and held his breath in case the Keeper decided to throw him out; but moments later he let out his anxiety. The only noise came from the direction of the Keeper's desk was the sound of his quill scratching the paper.

He gently unfastened the clasps, the S' turning into a C'. The castle library was never totally silent much to the Keepers displeasure, a living, breathing castle never stops for a moment, and even though the library was tucked away high in one of the turrets, some noise still carried but now a silence descended around him.

Opening the book, Villian managed to gasp without it leaving his lips. His eyes rested on a page. A red dragon, as vibrant as the day it was painted. He couldn't comprehend how something so old had never faded. Tentatively, he ran his hand over the painting, where layers and layers of paint formed the raised touch of the individual scales. The dragon enclosed was at the centre of circles of colour, which swirled in the light, as if they were fluid, a living fire and not solid. He had never seen anything like this in his life.

He closed his eyes, imagining the dragons soaring through the air. The noise and excitement of riding at the head, as King, after he'd saved Arcus and he'd brought back the dragons to restore peace as he'd promised his mother.

"Daydreaming again, lad. You will never make a king, hiding in dusty rooms all day long. You need to get your head out of books and get to the war council. A meeting you're late for, as usual!"

Inwardly Villian groaned. His father's aide never gave him a moment's peace, and he knew he would be only too pleased to tell his father where he'd found him, yet again.

Villian hunched over the book so Baynard couldn't see it.

"I shall be along shortly, Baynard. Please tell my father I'm sorry for the delay." He hoped his quiet clipped tones were enough to tell him he wasn't welcome.

The aide took another look at him, bowed sarcastically and left.

Villian sighed, if his father had seen him behave in such a way – he would have killed him on the spot, aide or not. He was surprised the Keeper hadn't said something to Baynard, but the evil man's reputation preceded him, and the Keeper might wake up to his library as a pile of ashes one early morning. Carefully, he closed the book, and after wrapping it in cloth he secured it in his leather backpack so the Keeper couldn't see it as he made his way out. Prince Villian nodded an apology and goodbye as he passed the desk, thinking his stealth skills were progressing, not realising The Keeper knew where every book was at any given time.

The Keeper chuckled to himself as the prince left. The boy was careful, he would give him that. If he were a simple librarian without the Magic, he was sure he wouldn't have known what Prince Villian was doing.

The Keeper put his quill down and stared at the place that had been his home for countless years. No-one had ever questioned his age; in the old times everyone knew why. But time had taken care of this problem. He was just always there. People probably thought his job was passed through generations. Sadly, it hadn't been his path in life to have a family to pass on this passion for history and the value of knowledge.

He missed Prince Villian's mother. She had been forward-thinking and inquisitive of the old ways. She believed in Magic and the old tales, even though Magic hadn't been seen in Arcus for thousands of years; ever since the dragons left. Only he, and a few others trusted by the dragons had passed on their powers, beliefs, and this last hope. He'd never told the queen this, but he suspected she knew what he was. That's why, at the last, she'd asked him to look out for her son and to keep him honest and on the path they knew he needed to take. Her death had been one of the hardest losses he'd endured over the years.

As Prince Villian left, so the hopes of this world and countless others went with him. The Keeper believed he was the boy they had been waiting for, and that the time was now. Which is exactly why he had let him find the book today. He would have liked to have taught him for a bit longer; but he knew time was against them. He prayed the boy was ready.

Chapter Six – Suntra

Bluewing waited high up in the sky. It was time to practice his silent dive. The General, his father, had recently taught them this manoeuvre, and he was keen to perfect it. Especially if it meant he would finally be better at something than Pathandon, his friend and number one competition.

He cleared his mind so Pathandon couldn't work out where he was. It was a skill a dragon had to learn from a young age; otherwise all the others would get annoyed when you spoke constantly, as he was apt to do.

There he was. Bluewing could see his friend searching for him. He concentrated on his dive. Pathandon was flying low over the sea, his head turning quickly, trying to find him.

Bluewing tipped and caught the natural currents which helped propel him faster to his target. His wings were tucked in tight, making his form as small as possible. The light from the sun behind him so that if his victim looked up, the light would shield his descent.

Faster and faster he dived; Bluewing loved combat.

He was seconds from Pathandon; this was going to work. A final tip of his wing to move into position. He had him. But right at the last second Pathandon tipped to the side and Bluewing didn't have time to stop his momentum and plunged straight into the sea.

Seconds later, he emerged, water cascading down his scales.

'Enjoy your dip, my friend?'

Bluewing could sense the mirth from Pathandon.

'What gave me away? I thought I had you then!'

'You forgot about your shadow on the water again. The General has told you many times, Bluewing. Until that point, I didn't know you were there. It has to be at the right time of the day to capture it perfectly.'

'Next time I will get you. That is a promise. I'm going to get in trouble now, it takes days to recover after a water dousing. My fire lessons are out, and we are so close to leaving.'

'You forgot to close your mouth again! You'll never learn Bluewing. Some help you will be in a battle.'

Bluewing knew he still had a lot to learn. But, in dragon terms, they were incredibly young. It could take dragons hundreds of years to learn the skills they had to start to learn since birth. They were still young in dragon years, but time was not on their side. All the younglings were excited at the prospect of an adventure; the Elders just looked worried all the time. Bluewing's father had been hard on them since birth. The Blues were known for their fighting ability; his father was the general of the army after all, and they were protectors of the royal dragons. The sense of duty was strong in them all.

Bluewing hoped that when they finally returned to Arcus, they would get to kill the evil Masters the King and Queen had told them about. Bluewing couldn't imagine letting one of the humans ride him though. It seemed so rude, as if they owned them somehow, or were their superior, when it was clear that dragons were superior to everything.

'Fancy a race?'

'Don't you want to practice your dive a few more times? Didn't the General say you needed to perfect it by the next session? It would go some way to impressing him so you don't get into too much trouble when they find out you cannot do your fire training.'

Pathandon was constantly practicing. He wanted to be the best, wanted to live up to the king's expectations. Even though Bluewing thought his grandfather really wanted them to just to be happy. He'd spotted King Pathanclaw on top of the mountains a few times; sometimes his mind had been unlocked and Bluewing had felt the sadness of responsibility. The loss of Pathandon's mother and father had been scary for them all. Had the allergy they'd spoken of travelled with Queen Silvarna when she'd been pregnant?

Perhaps they shouldn't have named his friend after his father, maybe the name was too much for the king and queen. Pathandon's father had been sickly his whole life and so the story went that everyone was surprised and elated when Maya had given birth to Pathandon. Soon after Pathandon was born, it was clear Maya wouldn't survive. Pathandon's father had lived long enough to see his son safe with his grandfather, then he'd flown away with his wife's body and, weak from his illness and the loss of his mate, had curled around her body and said the words that were a dragons' right, and chosen to die. No dragon could live in peace without their mate.

Bluewing was glad the sickness of his father hadn't passed to his friend. Pathandon was as strong as they came, very much like the king. One day, he would rule the family and Bluewing would be his General. He would be the best general a king had ever had. He would lead armies and destroy anyone he was honoured to protect. He puffed out his chest. One day he would be as big as his father...

Bluewing roared as Pathandon caught him in a full death roll. *'Daydreaming again, my friend. It will be your undoing.'*

The pair plummeted to the ground. Pathandon gripped him tight and Bluewing couldn't get his wings out. His friend had him, and he knew it. He would have to surrender or risk another plunge into the sea.

'You know that I've already been doused once today, don't you? So, if I don't surrender, it means you will have to plummet into the ocean with me, thus you will not be able to use your fire.'

'That is a good point my friend and one I have considered.'

'Oh yes, smart one. How pray, are you, going to do that? Even the General cannot pull that one off. That's why it's called a death roll.'

'You're about to find out my friend.'

The sea was fast approaching. As they reached the point of no return, Bluewing felt Pathandon's grip loosen, but before he had chance to spread his wings and fly clear, Pathandon's powerful legs caught Bluewing full in the chest, and he used this momentum to launch his body into the air. Bluewing hit the water hard, to the laughter of his friend.

'That was some move your grandson pulled off. Perhaps he should be teaching the younglings and not me. I've obviously lost the edge I once had.'

Pathanclaw turned to look at his friend and General, Battlewing, *'You still have a lot to teach them. I must say that was an impressive move though. Do you think we have made a wise choice only taking Pathandon and not your son as well? Bluewing will not like being left out, and they have trained all their lives. Maybe we should take him?'*

The General considered his friend's wisdom. It made sense to have a backup, and initially he thought it would be best if the four of them made the dangerous journey, but they needed someone to stay behind and lead the others through. Silvarna would be the one to take on this task; but a Blue was always present at the side of the King or Queen. They could not break tradition, not now, not ever.

'No, we have gone over this numerous times, my King. My son will stay to help lead our families through. It is our way. We need Pathandon to come; the magic is strong in him and we will need that. He also needs to know the dangers. If I had my way you wouldn't be going though.'

'Are you saying I'm too old to do this?'

They'd had many heated arguments when the subject first came up. But Pathanclaw had insisted it was his role and his alone. He had the power to open the portal and take them through. There were also things he hadn't told them. He knew the day would come. But not yet. Not yet.

'I wouldn't dare say such a thing about my King.' But there was laughter in the General's thoughts, as well as an acceptance of desire to argue this point again.

'You have said it yourself, and Silvarna has impressed on me numerous times that if you do not return in one piece to lead us back to Arcus, then my presence would not be welcome here on Suntra.'

'My wife is a force!'

'Her Majesty is. But the Queen is normally right as well. We need your grandson's power. We don't know what we will face when we leave here. He will be king one day and he needs to learn what that means and to earn the respect to lead.'

Neither of them mentioned that if it didn't work, the Royal Red Dragons would be no more. Failure was not an option either of them acknowledged. The path had been set and they would make it work. The humans needed them. Their future depended on it.

Chapter Seven – Luminosa

Thanan relaxed into his position high at the top of the cave. He tried not to look down at the blackness. His friend Tobias lived so high that the other colours didn't penetrate this far. He had come to enjoy his time travelling through the caves and used it to prepare his mind for his training; to form questions in his mind; trying to remember everything Tobias was teaching him, so he could be ready when the day came.

As usual, the session with his trainer, teacher and mentor started with him asking a question, which they then discussed. Even though Thanan was fairly sure that Tobias knew the answer, he rarely simply told him. In fact, in the five years he had been training, he didn't think Tobias had answered one directly.

When he was settled in the chair, they started.

"So, Thanan. What's your first question today?"

"I wondered if the rumours about this world being filled with dragons and humans living together were true?"

"Ah, that's an interesting question, Thanan, and one you have asked in different ways many, many, times before. We have spoken about the worlds that live in different times. Do you think it would be possible?"

"Well, Star has her Dragon, and they seem to live together okay."

"Yes, but Dragon has been made through magical ability and not born. Do you think that makes a difference?"

Thanan thought about it a few minutes as was expected of him. Tobias was a strict teacher. He couldn't abide guesses. Each answer had to be considered.

"Yes, it must. Dragon is linked to Star in a different way. Do you know if real dragons still exist, Tobias?"

"I think in worlds filled with Magic anything is possible."

Thanan smiled, still not an answer. He supposed an experienced trainer needed to make his pupil come by the conclusions himself. But it was frustrating never to get an answer. He had learned the hard way that life was tough, and more often than not he had to work to obtain anything and sometimes even that was not enough. Often, he'd felt like giving up, but something inside him wouldn't let the weakness to fail take hold.

"Can we move on from talking about dragons again? Think of another question, Thanan."

He only ever wanted to talk about dragons. He was still annoyed when he found out that he would be trained in magic rather than having a magical creature. He'd been only five when he'd arrived here and seven when he'd been chosen by Tobias. He couldn't really remember his past life. As with children, he'd just accepted where he was. Some of the children said it was a great privilege to be sent here; that they were training to take part in a great change across the universe. As usual though, they were told nothing of use, and most of the children were just repeating stories of others before them.

"Come on, Thanan. Concentrate. Please. I can hear your mind wandering all over the place. Focus."

"Sorry, Tobias. Too much to think about. Okay, so Star and I were wondering how big the camp is."

"That is not worthy of you, Thanan. You can find that out for yourself, although I urge you to be cautious. As you know the Masters are not forgiving."

"I would like to know where the children go after they turn thirteen..." Thanan interrupted Tobias before he could protest, as this was another question, he'd asked many times. "I have a theory and I would like to discuss it with you."

"Go ahead, Thanan."

"So, I've been thinking that a change must happen in children when they turn thirteen as they all leave with no exceptions, and that this must be a magical change, because the Masters are only interested in magic. I haven't worked out if that change is for the better or worse yet. I think that we are taken to another place and maybe the magic is taken from us or used for something else."

"Why do you think the Masters would do this, Tobias?"

"Because they are evil."

"How do you know they are evil?"

"Come on, Tobias, they steal children and keep us in the camp and make us do training every day. We are not allowed to leave."

"Do you not enjoy your training?"

"Well yes, but..."

"Are you not well fed?"

"Yes, but..."

"How do you know you've been stolen?"

Thanan had to think about this. "Other children said they remembered their families. Star said she remembered her parent's crying."

"Do you think she could have been mistaken?"

Thanan felt angry. Why would any parent give up their child willingly? Although what did he know about parents? He couldn't remember his, and he'd only heard things from the children about their vague memories. No child ever arrived older than five and Thanan had his suspicions that something happened to them to make them forget. The memories were like dreams that disappeared as you woke, unable to grasp the threads of a story. He felt confused.

"Maybe, I suppose. But some children cry for days until they get punished and quickly learn to shut up. That must mean that even if our parents gave us away, they wouldn't want us to live like this. Most of us have been hurt by the Masters at some point. I don't care what you say about where we came from, that isn't right."

"You're correct, Thanan. The way you children are treated sometimes is not the way it should be."

"Then why ask me those questions and make me think I'm wrong?"

"Because questioning what you believe, and thinking about the world and the many possibilities is what I'm here to teach you. You must look at what is behind the decisions others make, not just at what you see before you. Do you think it is so clear that people are either good or evil? Could a person not be both?"

"I suppose they could. I think Star would happily kill anyone to protect her friends or others who were vulnerable. But the Masters are not children. They should know better, be better."

"Why do you allow the Masters to do this?"

For a moment Thanan thought he'd gone too far. He hadn't even thought about it before the words appeared. He felt awful that he might upset his friend and teacher. He could feel the emotion from Tobias.

"We all have roles in this great universe, Thanan. Some are simple and some are great. To interfere with what we are would be a great mistake. I can only teach willing and receptive people like you and hope that you go out into the world and spread this knowledge and goodness. It's not so easy for me to leave. As you can see."

Thanan smiled. He knew that Tobias couldn't leave this cave. This was his home, and what could a worm really do against the Masters – even a giant worm. But, what could a boy do? How could he stop them hurting and stealing the children? Tobias knew everything, surely, he could use that knowledge to stop them.

"Where do you think all the children go, Tobias?"

"Some knowledge has to be earned Thanan, and some knowledge is too big to know all at once. There are many steps you need take to understand this world, and time, and people. You have to walk the path and take many journeys before you can understand its many routes."

"No answer, as usual." Thanan sighed, but with a smile on his lips this time.

He could feel the answering smile from Tobias. It was going to be bad enough to leave his friend. He couldn't bear to leave with bad feeling. He wasn't sure why he'd said those things. No, that wasn't true. He was scared.

"You're a clever boy, Thanan. I wouldn't have picked you if I didn't think so. It's been a long time since I've had a friend to talk to. I know that you're frustrated by my answers, or lack of them as you keep saying, but I believe in you to find these answers in time, by yourself, and to deal with them when you've journeyed longer in your life. Some paths are not clear even when the light shines on them."

"I'm clever enough to know you're ignoring my questions again!" With that the lightness was in their friendship again and the harsh words forgotten.

Thanan left the cave shortly after and thought about everything they had spoken about as he made his way into the camp. Tobias had insisted he use this time to reflect. Despite leaving as friends, Thanan felt confused and frustrated. Tobias had been more vague than usual. Surely what was happening here wasn't right? Surely someone had to stop the Master? Was it possible that he was going to be the one that did; one day, after he'd left this world? Would he come back and save everyone? Stop the Masters and rescue all the others he'd left behind?

He kicked at the ground hitting a big rock by accident, making him cry out in pain.

"Oh look, the little baby is crying. Did you hurt your little foot, poor baby?"

He didn't need to turn to know it was Triana following him. He ignored her and carried on down the path. He'd learnt that retaliation only came back on him tenfold where she was concerned; she had the Masters favour. He quickened his pace ignoring the laughter behind him. It was later than he thought and the black of night would be upon him before he reached his hammock. He never thought of it as home. He clenched his fist. One day he would find his home.

Chapter Eight – Arcus

Villian left the library and before he turned his attention to the war council, he went to visit the castle smithy, his precious cargo safe in his rucksack. His father would berate him anyway so what did it matter? His friend, the blacksmith, was a brute of man with a booming voice; everyone knew when Ironhand was around. Villian was sure Ironhand wasn't his real name, but who would argue with someone who had arms larger than a child's head, and muscles on muscles?

He held tightly to the straps of his backpack. Like most of his clothes and items, it had been specially made, a prince's privilege. He felt the burden of the book, both in weight and importance. He wasn't sure it was wise to show it to Ironhand, but no-one else knew the compositions of metals and precious stones like he did. It was worth the risk. Ironhand was loyal, he was sure he wouldn't mention it to anyone.

Villian had pestered him from a young age to be allowed into his smithy. Finally, he'd relented but it had come with strict instructions after Villian had burnt his arm. Ironhand's normally red face had paled – worried about the repercussions from the King. True to his word, Villian had lied about how it had happened and their trust in each other was sealed.

Walking through the streets, people bowed their head in acknowledgement. Unlike the rare days his father walked the streets, everyone had a smile for the young prince. Villian knew this was mainly due to his mother. She had been loved by the people, and even now people mourned her loss.

The streets were buzzing with life. Villian noticed that there were many more people entering the castle; subjects he didn't recognise. The farmers were leaving their lands and looking to the safety of the castle. This would add flames to the rumours about the impending battle. Villian hoped they would be ready. These people deserved to live in peace. His stride grew firmer. This gave him even more purpose. They would look to him and not his father and their ancient ways of battle.

He knew his father would be angry that he didn't use his guards; his mother had refused to allow him to have one by his side as a child. He'd heard the arguments between them. Villian was forever grateful now that he had so much freedom, as he wouldn't have chance to visit his friends in secret. He suspected Baynard was often on his tail and now it was getting closer to leaving, he was ever more cautious. Hopefully, the odious snitch was in the war council, no doubt pointing out his absence.

Even after all these years, the heat and noise of the smithy took his breath away. He'd neglected his friend for a while as he'd been working with Raykan on the quest. Villian felt a little guilty, but it couldn't be helped. Villian's muscles were in part due to the teachings of Ironhand as well as the practice with the Master Sword.

"Still have more brawn than brains then, Ironhand?"

"You still have neither, young Prince." Ironhand put down his hammer and gathered Villian in a bear hug that lifted him off his feet and almost crushed him.

"Nice to see you, too. Do you mind not breaking my bones? My father will have your rather large head."

Ironhand's forge boomed with his laughter. He let go and slapped him on the back, but luckily Villian was braced for it or else it would have knocked him to the floor.

"It's been a while, my Prince. Too busy chasing after those ladies? I hear that the announcement is due any day now. I've made you some shackles for your special day."

No-one else would get away with speaking to him like this. Somehow this smith was classless. He could talk to the lowliest peasant on the streets and to the highest born. It was no matter to him, he only cared about metal and precious stones. He also knew his value.

"Thank you, my friend. I will bear that in mind when the joyous occasion arrives."

He was rewarded with a deep chuckle, like a volcano about to erupt.

"Right, what can I do for you, young Prince? Some of us have swords to make. There's a battle brewing if you didn't know."

"Oh, I know all about it alright. I'm on my way to the war council, where everyone will say a lot but do very little. Unlike me."

Ironhand arched his large eyebrow. Everything about Ironhand was large.

"Do I need to worry?" He sounded worried, which was unusual. Villian thought nothing could faze this bear of a man.

"No. But, I do need your help with something."

"BOY." Ironhand shouted into the forge, making Villian jump. A second later his apprentice turned up, looking petrified as usual.

"We're off to the tavern. Cover here while I'm gone, and if this place goes up in flames, my boy, you better run far and hide well."

With that, he strode out, Villian following with a smirk, but feeling slightly sorry for the boy.

Settled into a room at the back of the tavern, Ironhand had cleared it before he entered. It wouldn't do well for Villian to be seen in such places. Villian didn't mind, he liked being amongst his people, but if his father got wind he was in a common tavern when he should be in the council there would be hell to pay. The tavern owner kept quiet – no-one would mess with Ironhand; not if you ever wanted any barrels making or horses shod, or beer drunk for that matter.

After taking a large gulp, which nearly amounted to the whole flagon of beer, Ironhand started proceedings. “Right, my Prince. What can I do for you?”

Villian took a deep breath. He knew he was taking a risk, not only for himself, but this could put Ironhand in danger.

“I’ve got something to show you, and I want you to tell me what kind of metal it is.”

“Seems simple enough.”

Villian reached into his backpack and took out the book. Setting it carefully on the table he ran his finger over the dragon clasps, his whole body tingling.

Ironhand stared at it before placing a large finger above the clasp. “Well, my boy, looks like I was right to be worried. You’re in greater danger than I thought.”

Chapter Nine – Suntra

It had been a hard day for them all. The General had trained them ruthlessly with no breaks. On and on it went. Practicing until their wings ached. Formations were the hardest for the younglings to learn. To allow no gaps, no opportunity for the enemy to see what lay behind them. The silver dragons would line up first. Their skills lay in hunting, their agility and eyesight better than any other of the families. They would search the ground until the prey was spotted. One tip of their body, a magic touch, and the sunlight would dazzle their prey with their mirror-like scales.

On the signal of the General they would part and fly to the back, and behind them the gold dragons would push forward. They were ferocious fighters, but they needed more of them. Only eleven of them remained; nine of them able to fight. The two elders had come through the portal, with ten others of their kind. But only ten had made it, and only two of them had borne one male dragon. But they were a force. Today, even the elders, past their fighting days, took up the outer positions, their presence spurring on the others in the practice.

The gold dragons gave way to the only four black dragons that had made it through. Their numbers never large, few were ever born. But the four were powerful, their magic derived through many thousands of years of study. They were the guardians of the gems. Pathanclaw likened them to the human monks. Their time was often spent in solitude and learning. But today, the sight of them brought the old memories back. Smaller than the rest of the dragons, Pathandon was already bigger than a full-sized black, but what power they had!

Next came the Blues, the royal protectors. The greatest number that had come through and borne children – but still only sons. They were thirteen strong, but in the formation lay the General, his wife Kyanite and taking up the head of the three, Bluewing, proud to be at the head, leading his family and protecting the Royal Reds. Bluewing's heart beat so fast he thought it would burst. He wished he could watch this from the ground where the rest of the dragons were learning the formations for battle.

The green dragons were never in the fight. Only two of their kind had made it through and they rarely interacted with the others. They slept deep in the mountains surrounded by gems, drawing their power and transferring this to the others. The purples had not been seen, they were by nature elusive and secretive, unusual traits for a dragon. They were made for magic and not for fighting. They had disappeared from Arcus many thousands of years ago, before the fighting started. The most mysterious of dragons. They were feared because they were unknown. Pathanclaw, the oldest of them, had only ever met one great purple dragon, back when the portal had been formed and the Festival of Time came to be.

The Blues tipped to the side and through the gaps came the Royal Reds. Flames bellowed from them as all the dragons roared their battle cry, shaking the very ground beneath them. It was a display not seen for thousands of years.

"AND AGAIN!" roared the General.

Bluewing and Pathandon passed each other as they took up their positions once again. This was the best day of their lives.

Chapter Ten – Luminosa

Thanan was struggling to sleep, his thoughts straying back to his lessons with Tobias. He was still frustrated. It made him think back to his first days in the camp, trying to delve into his memory and find questions Tobias wouldn't answer.

When they had first been gathered for training, Thanan had been excited to start the day. He thought he might have been five when he arrived here, but he couldn't be sure. He'd kept to himself until the arrival of Star, and later Pol. He'd never fitted in with any of the groups, but he didn't mind, a lot of the children looked lost.

He'd tried to take note of when children arrived and what ages they were, to see if he could see a pattern. But either there wasn't one or he couldn't see it. Some of the children had been kept somewhere else for what sounded like years before they were brought to the camp. Even though he preferred his own company, when new children arrived, he always tried to make them feel at ease. He'd ask them questions to try and find out what they remembered. Mostly, it amounted to nothing.

On the day he'd met Star, he'd seen the new arrivals turn up, most looking dazed and confused; other than one, Star; who would become his best friend. Someone said she looked like an Amazonian goddess, but Thanan didn't know what that was until he'd spoken to Tobias about it. He only knew she was tall, had attitude and that he was slightly scared of her.

One day about ten children were in the training room. Thanan didn't particularly like being with the Masters as they creeped him out. Their long black flowing hooded cloaks and whispered cutting tones didn't make the session fun, unless you loved learning Magic of course, which Thanan did.

They were given tests to do. A situation to face, and the Masters would watch to see how they reacted. This decided which area they were sent to study. They had seemingly been impressed by Thanan's ability to do some of the more difficult tests, apparently this meant he would fare well with the formation of complex spells.

Star and Thanan said it would have been nice to have trained together, but he knew Star's ultimate goal was to have a magical dragon, and she was too flighty to retain information which was needed to create spells. He'd tried to describe it to her one day. The best he could come up with was that it was like picking up lots of items and juggling them above his head, before placing them back where you found them but in a different order. Star had snorted at his explanation.

It had been Star's first day, and everyone had gathered when it was time for the newly tested children to come out of the testing rooms. Nothing much happened in camp due to the strict rules, so this was always a good event. Thanan saw Triana turn up and knew instantly she was going to make trouble for him.

Normally they couldn't do much on the outside due to the lack of magic allowed in the camp. But on test day they were given a 'free' day, so magic was allowed; although still monitored by the Masters he suspected, unless you were their favourite like Triana.

Thanan had sensed that Triana was preparing a spell, and no doubt it would be something directed at him. He saw her hand stretch out. She was forming a fire ball; great. Thanan mentally prepared the blocking spell, creating the complex patterns that would shield him and others around him. Just as he was about to release it, Star came along, and quickly realising the situation, pushed Triana over; purely by accident, she'd promised the Masters. She simply hadn't seen her, and she'd been rushing to get into the right place; worried about letting them down. She was very convincing.

Triana had landed on her own fireball and one of her friends used the water spell with complete effectiveness due to them being unable to modify the torrent of water that nearly drowned the gasping girl in the process.

Thanan hadn't had time to thank Star as the Masters took control and they were all sent back to their hammocks. It was a few days later that their paths crossed again.

The new children had only been in camp for a few days and they were huddled together, while Triana frightened them half to death talking about what the Masters were going to do to them, and how if they strayed too far the Suckers would drain all their blood. Thanan had been about to interrupt and take the consequences when Star stepped in again.

"Why don't you leave them alone, you horrible girl?" Star was face to face with Triana.

Triana wasn't used to being spoken to like that, everyone else was too scared to put her in her place, but she soon recovered, ready to put this up-start in her place.

"Why don't you mind your own business, you blue haired freak?"

Star moved forward ever so slightly, her face nearly touching Triana's. Thanan saw Triana flinch, and he smiled. Everyone held their breath and she whispered, "If you don't leave these children alone right now, I will sneak into your shack tonight and cut off all your hair."

Triana's hand went to her luscious, long, curly brown hair, which she made one of her minions comb for her every night.

"If you do that, I will pay you back, don't you worry about that." Triana hissed through gritted teeth, careful not to let the others overhear.

"Well, tell you what. You walk away and leave these children alone, and I won't cut your hair off, and for the record, I wouldn't care if you cut mine off, because I would still be a nice person with or without hair, unlike you."

Triana could see she had met her match. To save face she shouted she had better things to do and stalked off, her friends following in her wake.

Star walked straight up to Thanan who was opened-mouthed at this point. He'd never heard anyone speak to Triana that way. Star leaned comfortably on his shoulder, being a head taller than him at the time, and said, "So, she's a piece of work. Anyone else I need to watch out for?"

Thanan had been so stunned that anyone wanted to speak to him, he didn't answer.

"Oh great, my new best friend cannot speak. Oh well, luckily, I have enough to say for both of us. Now come on let's get something to eat. I'm starving."

From that day to this they'd been best friends. Their relationship had developed over the years and as Thanan had grown taller than Star, she would naturally defer to him if only to keep her out of trouble, as she was predisposed towards action, rather than words. She certainly had plenty of those as well; she just didn't think before they left her mouth.

The day Pol had joined them had been a strange day. The Masters had been on edge for days. Everyone in the camp knew something was going on. One morning they had woken up to Pol being in Star's hut. She'd been sitting in the corner, her dungarees and long feathery boots seeming to engulf her small form. Star had, of course, immediately tried to engage her in conversation only to find out she didn't speak.

Pol had followed Star around all morning, until break time when she joined Thanan for snacks. This was also when they discovered much to their shock, that not only could she gender-shift but she was also telepathic. Star was totally weirded out and demanded to know if Pol could hear all her thoughts. Pol stated they could only hear what Star wanted them to hear. Then Star demanded that Pol keep switching between male and female, staring into her eyes to watch them change from purple to orange, until Thanan had told them they should stop before Pol fainted, and that it was totally not a nice thing to do, even though he was also fascinated.

They'd never met anyone who could change from being a boy to a girl with a blink of an eye. Star had asked if they could transform into anything else, but it didn't seem so. Until they knew Pol better it was tricky to know if they were a girl or a boy unless you knew the signs. Staring directly into their eyes to check the colour was a bit rude, but after time they noticed the subtle changes to their posture and Pol's personality was different. Star and Thanan started calling Pol 'them' and 'they' rather than 'he' and 'she' as it suited Pol better. It was strange at first, but then became normal. Of course, when Triana heard about Pol's ability, she had something to say about it, but Star soon put an end to that.

The other children gave Pol a wide berth. Even to the children here, Pol seemed strange. All the children were forbidden to talk about where they came from, but it was clear they were not from the same place. Even the same planet. One day Star had asked one of the other children, and Thanan had been worried when she hadn't appeared for their usual mealtime meets. Two days later she had appeared, pale and withdrawn, not wanting to talk. Gradually after a few days, she returned to her old bossy and confident ways. But she never asked another child about where they came from and was the first to warn the children to keep quiet.

Thanan sighed. This place was all he'd ever consciously known. As with many nights in the past he'd tried to remember a time before. He thanked the Gods that Star had turned up and later Pol. It could be a lonely place without a friend. Some children lacked purpose or didn't pass the tests and would go missing before their thirteenth name day, never to return.

Eventually, Thanan fell asleep. He didn't hear Pol come into his hut and touch his forehead. The worry lines that had stayed with him in slumber, relaxed. He woke up feeling refreshed and ready for the day; he'd made peace with the troubles of yesterday.

Chapter Eleven – Arcus

Villian had hidden the book in his chamber before making his way to endure the wrath of his father. The war council had been predictably the same. Men stood around shouting at each other and not coming up with any sensible plans. Villian had learned to keep his opinions to himself, which would further infuriate his father, after his only son was extremely late.

Baynard had smirked when he entered; it clearly pleased him to know that Villian would get a dressing down later. Just the sight of his father's aide made Villian angry. He didn't know why his father kept the slimy worm around. His greasy hair and unkempt look wasn't fitting for the highest of tables.

The reports made for grim reading. The army of their enemy were gathering their forces at a quicker rate than they'd anticipated. Within months, the army could be on their doorstep. Every effort was being made to strengthen the castle. Provisions were being stored, and they'd increased the production of weapons – as Villian had seen earlier. But there were strange reports which left the king uneasy. These had not yet reached the ears of his council.

When the subject of weapons came up, Baynard had said casually, "I'm sure you know all about this, Prince Villian. You spend lots of time in that area checking they are not slacking on their duties."

Villian's eyed narrowed. He had to be more careful. Baynard had a lot of spies in the castle. He couldn't afford for anyone to know what he was doing. He would need to warn his friends to be more careful.

"That's right, Baynard. I take my father's interests and the realms very seriously. Nothing makes people work harder than the sight of their Prince."

His father had acknowledged his commitment, and Villian had smiled at Baynard. He, in turn, scowled, knowing his ruse to get Villian in further trouble had fallen on deaf ears.

This praise hadn't stopped his father being enraged afterwards, and he'd had to stand and listen in silence as he lectured him about his responsibilities to the council. To talk back was insolent, and pointless. His stepmother looked on with some sympathy. They had never been close, and he felt the pain of her barrenness. But he had always been respectful and understood his father's need to marry again. It was probably the reason Villian hadn't been banished. He was the true heir, and his father believed in the lineage of name and blood.

Villian had been thoughtful throughout the war council and offered little opinion, hence the wrath of his father afterwards.

In his bedchamber Villian paced the room, waiting for the right time to sneak out and head to Raykan's to find out more about the dragon book, as Villian was in no doubt it was the one they had been searching for, especially after what Ironhand had said.

The bell rang for evening supper and after waiting another hour, sure in the knowledge the food and drink would be flowing, he took his familiar route out of the castle. Changing into commoner's clothing once again, and hiding his dark long hair, he cautiously made his way to Raykan's home, constantly checking to see if he were being followed. It was a skill he'd developed over the years. He was his father's son in that regard, and his hunting and tracking skills were second to none, knowing that Baynard had his spies made him ever more cautious and he double-backed a few times.

Villian had a whole castle to call home, but he preferred Raykan's small hut in the woods. The fire blazed all year round, the light and warmth of the sun never penetrating the dense woods. Villian didn't know how his friend could stand fire after the damage it had inflicted on his face and body. It made him ashamed to think his father had done this to such a kind and learned man.

"About time, Son. Where have you been?"

Raykan had called him 'son' from the first day he'd found Villian reading a stolen book in the woods. They had become firm friends, and Raykan's quiet authority made this address seem natural.

"The war council went on longer than it should, as was usual, and so the evening feast was delayed, and I have the feeling that Baynard is watching me, so I was more careful than I normally would be."

Raykan scowled. He looked twice as scary because of the scarring to his face. He'd had dealings with Baynard in the past and disliked him more than Villian did.

"You need to be extra careful, son. You know how devious and treacherous that odious man can be."

"I will. Never mind that, I've found the book!"

Raykan used his staff to raise himself from the chair by the fire. Villian had never asked him about the staff. He thought it was the bone of a dragon, but he didn't want to ask in case it made him sound stupid. It made Raykan seem even more intriguing and sometimes the knowledge of something stripped away its mystery.

Villian settled into his chair near the large desk that made up most of the room. His friend had no bed, just a chair that he slept in. The walls were covered from floor to ceiling with books. A large fireplace dominated one side with all manner of animals, furs and herbs in various stages of concoction.

He'd once asked Raykan why he didn't have a bigger place. He'd said he'd calculated the optimum distance required so that he wasn't wasting time walking from one side to the other.

This was all he needed. Well, and his spectacles, without which he wouldn't be able to see a dragon if it landed on his head; his words. Villian suspected it was to save him walking; he could see the pain in his face when they collected herbs from the surrounding wood. Raykan's cloak covered his body, but if the scarring was anything like his face, Villian wondered at his ability to stand.

Villian laid the book on the table and stood back, proud of his achievement, happy to please Raykan, excited that his quest would be starting soon. It hadn't come a moment too soon. If their plans were to work Villian needed to leave soon, and to do that, Raykan had said they needed the book.

His friend's face said it all. As he suspected, this was the book they had been searching for. After all these years, it was finally back with its rightful owner. Raykan felt his eyes fill, something he'd thought he'd forgotten how to do. He almost dare not touch it. His shaking hands hovered above it and he closed his eyes, feeling the memories.

"It is the right one?" Villian asked, breaking the silence.

"Yes, Son. Yes, it is."

"Brilliant. So, what do we do now?"

The boy was excited. As was his right. Excitement was made for a king's son. Raykan had felt the same feeling but knew his part in this tale was nearly done. His long life had led to this moment. This boy. He had played his part, and like any good guardian, the day had come to let go.

"Well, what are you waiting for? Make a drink before we start," Raykan said gruffly, to avoid Villian hearing the emotion in his voice. But Villian knew his friend too well.

"I have people to make my drinks. Princes do not make drinks for commoners."

Villian ducked as Raykan's staff swung towards his head. He laughed, as he moved the few steps to the stove to get their drinks. He felt alive. He knew the quest he had been working towards was about to begin. If it got him out of marrying Lady Cartina then all the better; he wanted to choose his own wife when the time came. Ironhand had spoken in jest but Villian wasn't ready for such responsibilities. His head was filled with great deeds, he had no interest in girls and weddings. These stupid rules of forced marriages would end when he was ruler.

They settled down at the desk. Many candles were lit around Raykan's room, and the fire provided much needed warmth.

Raykan finally crossed the chasm of space and caressed the top of the book. His eyes closed once again, remembering the feel of the dragon these scales belonged to. His old friend. It made him feel young again and at the same time as ancient as his years. He was ready to rest.

"Is it made of what I think it is?" Villian asked, dragging him from his youth.

"Dragon scale. Yes, my boy. Proof if the heathens of today needed any. Dragons do exist."

A shiver ran through Villian. He knew they existed, and of course he believed. His years of teachings by Raykan had left him in no doubt. But to touch a dragon, it was more than even a prince could dream of.

"The clasps are made from dragon blood."

Raykan looked sharply at him, "How do you know that?"

Villian looked smug, "You're not the only one that knows things, Raykan. I'm a Prince, it's my duty to know more than others."

"Oh, don't give me that, Son. But I will admit that I'm impressed that you know," Raykan turned his formidable gaze on him. "Who told you?"

Villian touched his nose, and added as Raykan was about to protest, "It's a friend. A trusted friend, I promise. I'm not stupid."

"Okay, we will say no more on the matter. Did 'this friend' tell you how it's made?"

"Yes, apparently when a dragon dies the blood can be turned into a precious metal, but only by the fire of another dragon and possibly some magic words."

Villian had been stunned when Ironhand had told him this. How he knew this he wouldn't let on. There was more to his smith friend than Villian knew. But in the telling the smith's frown had deepened.

"This path that you're on is dangerous, my Prince. I will not tell you to stop, as I know you wouldn't listen. But be incredibly careful who you trust with this information."

"Your friend is very well informed."

Raykan was reluctant to open the book. He needed to be alone when he discovered its contents again. He knew what lay within. This was the key. Now he would have the means to send this brave young prince on an adventure that he might never return from, and if he didn't return, Arcus as they knew it, would be lost.

Putting the book to one side, much to Villian's surprise and annoyance, they went back to the maps. Villian thought he knew them off by heart as he'd been studying them long enough. A prince should know more than just the land his royal feet trod on was all the response he would get. Sighing, he looked down, but it wasn't a map he was familiar with. Not a map of Arcus. This was somewhere else.

He looked up. It was Raykan's turn to look smug.

"To work, my Son. To work."

After a few hours Raykan sent him on his way, telling him to return in two days' time so they could go through their final plans.

Villian was weary when he got back to the castle. It had been a long, but exciting day. He changed into his finery and made his way to his chambers. The guards nodded. It was not unusual for him to return late. As the guards closed Villian's door, a man left the shadows.

Chapter Twelve – Suntra

After the battle practice a few days previously, Pathanclaw had spent the day training the youngsters. It was something he enjoyed, and he didn't get the chance to do it as often as he would like. Watching them get their wings and their first breath of fire was a delight to behold and he knew his kin of old would be proud.

Their line was not as strong as it should be. Pathandon would be a great king one day but he needed a mate, and with no female dragons having been born since coming here, it worried him every moment. He was tired; he knew he would need his old strength to get through the next stage in the history of the dragons. The Magic given to him all that time ago was finally nearing its end. He had lived longer than any other dragon, and he was grateful he'd been given the chance to see his kind thrive again. He needed to complete his final task and take his family back to their home world. For the millionth time he wondered if he was making the right decision. Maybe they should stay here, but they couldn't thrive without females. They were in danger and needed them. He knew, or he hoped, that not of all the female dragons could have perished. He, like the other elders, felt their presence somewhere. In their haste to leave Arcus, many must have got separated and surely not all had perished. He also felt the pull of the humans' peril.

It was the end of a long day and as usual they finished with a story. Tonight, it was his grandson's turn to tell the old story of how humans and dragons came to be.

Silvarna looked on proudly, as Pathandon told the group how thousands of years ago his ancestor was saved by a human, and the magical bond was created. Up until that point humans hadn't been aware dragons existed. They'd used their magic to shield themselves from the humans, never letting their presence be known. But once the friendship was formed, it held strong through time and place. The humans were in danger now and the dragons needed to make sure they did all they could to help.

Queen Silvarna had encouraged Pathandon to tell the story about the day the dragons left Arcus. Her grandson had delivered it with the odd nudge from his friend Bluewing. The story told that dragons had become allergic to humans and had to leave the world before they were all destroyed. It was the only secret Pathanclaw had ever withheld from his wife. Buried deep within his mind, too dangerous to share with any of his kind, the truth of how it had come about, the shame he still felt. This shame drove him to succeed and repent as the humans did.

He cleared his mind and concentrated on his grandson. Ever headstrong, Pathandon had joined a group beyond his years but not his capabilities. He was a fast learner, and often took advantage of his lineage when his grandfather wasn't looking, although this had lessened as the time to leave grew closer.

Losing Pathandon's parents; his beloved son and wife had been more than he thought they could bear. But he owed it to his son to see his grandson didn't succumb to the same fate. Luckily, Panthadon had survived and thrived under his grandparents' love and attention and there was no sign of the illness that caused his parents' demise. Silvarna was constantly complaining that he indulged him, but he knew she did the same. He thought again about the human names they adopted. He had the knowledge of the old names somewhere, but even a dragon's great memory failed sometimes.

Melancholy had taken hold. Pathanclaw stretched his wings each the length of two houses at last count, now so long ago since his friend had measured them. His scales glinted in the glorious sun as it started to close on the day. Story finished, he took flight to try and fly off the melancholy. He dropped out of the sky, high above the plains and swooped down across the river, his wing barely touching the water, the ripples from his powerful wings making the water dance with patterns.

"You're too old for those kinds of moves, my darling." Silvarna, was by his side, keeping pace.

"This old dragon still has a few moves; don't you worry, my Queen."

"Oh really, let's see about that..."

Silvarna dipped to her left and pulled a daring move through a gap in the snow-capped mountains.

"Impressive darling, I didn't know you still had it in you. It looks like you have some fans."

The king and queen couldn't often go out without being noticed, especially when they were showing off for all to see. The younglings were preparing to take flight, no doubt wanting to join in this rare show.

"Race?" Silvarna asked, her voice clear in his mind.

"I thought you would never ask. Let's show these youngsters how it's done."

Pathanclaw and Silvarna spent the next few hours flying over what would soon become their old home. They fed in the mountains, and as was their way, they were respectful of the animals they hunted. They had let the younglings catch them up and fly for a little while, but they were approaching their last few days together. A few beats of their adult wings soon took them out of reach of the younglings and they soon gave up, content to go back and brag about flying with them.

He'd come to love this world. It was generous with its gifts. It was so much like Arcus, it would be so easy to stay and live until the end of his days. But, not only were they running out of time, the Festival of Time being the easier way to travel; but they could not go on forever without female younglings. Soon they would need females for the younglings, and for their species to survive. It wasn't only the humans who needed saving.

Too soon they were back. Pathanclaw summoned his General and friend, Battlewing. After finalising plans to leave in two days, he spent his time practising the ancient spells which would give him to power to leave this world and create a link. If all went to plan, he could lead his family back to salvation of the humans and a peaceful life, something his parents had wished for from the moment they'd had to leave. He hoped his friend had been successful in his plans. Their very lives depended on it.

He'd spent many hours training his grandson in the old magic, teaching him how to create a spell. The portal could only be opened with the most powerful of magic. Pathandon certainly had the power, but they had run out of time and he had to hope his grandson would be able to return them if anything happened to him. Pathanclaw hoped it would not be needed. He hoped he would manage to find his old friends. Could they still be alive? He knew magic had the ability to prolong a human's life; some even said they could live as a long as a dragon. He hoped beyond hope that this was true. He would love to see his friend just one last time.

Chapter Thirteen – Luminosa

"Will you stop that!" Thanan said angrily.

"But Dragon has to practice. How's she going to learn how to attack someone if she doesn't keep trying?" Star shouted.

Thanan hated their free magic days in camp. It was complete chaos, which was something the Masters normally avoided. Thanan thought they were secretly watching and seeing the level of powers the children truly had. Some of the children weren't stupid and didn't always show their abilities and strengths.

Star wasn't one of these, she was trying to make Dragon the strongest creature there. Already Dragon had begun to breathe fire; accidentally burning one of the food bushes down, much to the dismay of the children. But it was very hit and miss. Star had been oblivious to the screams of the children; she'd been delighted that Dragon had worked out how to breathe fire. Well, she admitted it was only a small flame and the rest of the attempts had just been puffs of smoke. But there had been flame!

During the night, when they thought no-one was looking, Pol crept to the food bush and with whatever strange powers they possessed, made the bush come back to life. Thanan was watching though. He studied his friend and wondered how they could formulate a spell to do that. He opened his mind to ask, but Pol just smiled shyly.

Star was lying on her front on the lush green carpet of moss, staring into Dragon's eyes, her long blue hair resting along her body, her long legs crossed at the ankle. The more Star worked with Dragon the bigger she became. It was as if the magic connection was feeding her.

"Right, Dragon. Now, you have to concentrate."

Dragon's head leaned to one side, her way of telling Star she was listening.

"I want you to practice the range of your fire. Okay?"

Dragon nodded her head.

"So, I'm going to lie here, and you have to practice not burning my face off?"

"Erm Star, I'm not sure that's such a good idea," Thanan said.

"It's okay, I totally trust her, we have been practising for ages now. If she does burn my face off, I'm sure Pol can fix me."

Thanan looked at Pol, who looked worried. Healing plants was one thing, humans quite another.

Star laughed, "If Pol cannot fix me, I will be the cool scarred dragon lady. Legends will talk about my beautiful looks ruined by fire, but my beauty will still shine through for all to see. The beauty will be in my soul. Men will fall at my feet desperate to marry this beautiful scarred princess."

At this point, Thanan and Pol were rolling around crying on the grass.

Dragon shot a small flame in their direction, narrowly missing Thanan's foot.

"Oi," he shouted.

Star laughed with delight, clapping her hands together. "See, look at the control she has already. Dragon could have easily burnt your foot off."

Star sat up and grabbed Dragon, hugging her tight, whispering what a good dragon she was. Dragon hadn't developed scales yet, the feathers on her body were still soft.

"Great control, I'm sure," Thanan said testily, his leather sandals hot to the touch. He was sure a few hairs on his leg had been singed. He could smell it.

Star was oblivious and had set Dragon back down to continue her lessons, lying back down in readiness. Rather

Star than him, Thanan thought, eyeing the searing hot flame shooting from the creature. He was surprised at how quickly she was learning. Either Star was a good teacher or Dragon a quick learner; either way they were clearly well suited to each other.

Thanan lay on the grass a good distance from the practising pair and closed his eyes so he could concentrate on using some of this precious time of free magic to form the spells he would need to leave this place. He had to be careful that he didn't show his hand, but there were a few he could practice without arousing suspicion.

In his mind he saw spells as layers of colour, they started with the colours of this world. Each one had to be placed in the right order or the spell didn't work. Somehow, he thought of the spell and the order was in his mind; he wasn't sure how he did it.

It started with gold. In his mind he saw a long ribbon which he laid in circles over and over again, until gradually he started weaving in silver, then sapphire blue, followed by emerald. At this point he had to interweave them. He thought of it like folding metal and hammering it into shape, but somehow more graceful. Once he had these firmly in place, he moved onto ruby, then his favourite purple tanzanite and finally to finish – the black of onyx. The black one was the trickiest to keep in form, it constantly wanted to shift from the shape he needed. Not all spells needed all the colours, many only required gold, silver and blue, like the levitation spell, he could form that in seconds now he had mastered the form.

Star looked at Thanan. He hadn't moved in hours, a clear indication he was working on his magic. She hoped he would be able to get quicker with practice. Once they left this awful place, they might need his magic. That was why she was working so hard with Dragon, she would need to protect them whilst they all developed their skills. Thanan would stay there until he had training again later that day, so Star left him alone.

Star thought Dragon needed a rest from her fire breathing, she'd done very well, and she only had a slight singe to her hair, which she decided looked very cool. It made them both tired if they practiced for too long.

"Right, Dragon. Before we finish, let's try something new."

Dragon held her gaze. Star still couldn't believe she'd ended up with a Dragon. She'd been desperate to have one. All the years of waiting for her magic creature had been worth it. She'd been envious at seeing others leave with their creatures; at one point she'd wondered if she really would ever get one, but her patience and wish were granted. Patience was something Tobias was always telling Thanan he needed, so maybe she had been rewarded. The Masters must have known she was capable, or they wouldn't have put her in that group. Maybe her stubbornness and need for a dragon had paid off. The children weren't sure how it worked, how their creatures were eventually chosen.

"Okay." Star placed her back against one of the tree stumps where everyone normally gathered for food time. She raised her knees to her chest and Dragon flew up to settle on them. He felt so much heavier, soon Dragon wouldn't be able to rest on her. Star would be sad when that day came, but the day she flew on Dragon would be the best day of her life.

Dragon's face was inches from hers, blue eyes staring into red ones. "So, we're going to try this. You need to think only about me, look at me. We need to have one mind."

Star figured that if she, Thanan and Pol could communicate with their minds, then why not with her Dragon?

They were given no guidance from the Masters on how to develop their creatures. Thanan had asked Tobias once and he'd said it was symbiotic and couldn't be taught. Obviously, he hadn't actually said this. He asked Tobias a series of questions until he'd interpreted the answer. Star couldn't see the point of having the most knowledgeable worm in the universe if it didn't tell you anything.

Star stared into Dragon's eyes until she felt her eyes blur, "Right, now close your eyes and talk to me."

Minutes later she opened her eyes. Nothing. Dragon wasn't even looking at her.

Star sighed, maybe it was too soon. It would be so much easier if she could communicate with her this way. When eventually they were free from this world, Dragon would be able to fly further than she could see.

Excited, something had just occurred to her. Maybe she could see through Dragon's eyes! How amazing would that be?

Dragon gave her a look.

"Okay, okay. Yes, I've had an idea. But you can go and fly around for a bit. Just don't be practising your fire without supervision."

Dragon took off, making Star jerk her legs. She was getting too heavy.

Star looked around, bored now and wanted to speak to the others. Thanan was still lying motionless and she didn't want to disturb him.

'Fancy exploring the forest, Pol? I'm bored.'

Pol appeared immediately in front of her making her jump. '*Pol!*' Star exclaimed, '*don't do that to me.*'

Pol held their hand out and pulled Star to her feet with a strength that belied their small form. Hand in hand they made their way into the forest. Star was happy Pol had decided to be a boy – they would have much more fun. They both loved the forest. Star didn't engage with the landscape quite in the same way as Pol. Even though it was a 'free time' they all had to be careful about letting others see Pol's real powers.

They spent a pleasant few hours wandering through the forest. Star never failed to marvel at the sheer size of the trees. Like Thanan, she couldn't really remember anything about where she came from before the camp, sometimes she had vague memories of people, but she didn't know if they were her parents. In her dreams she sometimes remembered seeing two people kneeling and crying in a stone room.

They had gone deep into the forest. Star wasn't sure they had ever gone this far and she was thinking about turning back. She didn't want to return in the dark, she hadn't brought Dragon with her and she'd left her phial of light in the hut. Pol stopped suddenly, and with her mind elsewhere, Star bumped into the back of them.

Pol pointed towards two large trees.

Star couldn't see what she was pointing to at first, the light was dazzling as it reflected off the sandy ground. She had to strain her eyes to see what Pol could see. Her mouth dropped open when she spotted what Pol had seen.

Suckers!

Chapter Fourteen – Arcus

Days later Villian made his way through the forest. It was his last few days in the castle and what a day. He'd spent his afternoon overseeing the battlements and checking on the supply of weapons after the feast. He was aware there were people to do this, but he felt it was his duty to know exactly what state their army was in. He'd also had a ruthless training session with his warriors; even he'd come away with a few bruises. Everyone was in high spirits after the ceremony.

He'd been excited to launch the new ship to their fleet. His new ship, built under his leadership. Most of the ship design he'd left to the experts, but he'd added the finishing touches.

The prominent lords and ladies had waited enthusiastically along with his father and stepmother. The port had been cleaned in honour of the one and only visit by Villian's father as he preferred to leave all matters to the council, rarely leaving the castle. Villian had been surprised when his father had accepted his request to attend.

Along the water's edge, people had been scrubbing and cleaning without too much success of masking the smell of the fish engrained into every piece of wood, stone and body that worked the harbour. It wasn't a necessity to walk through this area to reach their war ships, but Villian thought it would be good for the people to realise who was keeping this castle alive, keeping them in the comfort they were used to, and whom they were ultimately fighting for.

Villian admitted it stank. In the end he'd given permission for scent bearers to lead the procession, as well as having them strategically placed along the route. For some of the subjects this would be their first view of the King, or Lords and Ladies for that matter, all dressed in finery most would never see or wear. They were fisher people who never left the harbour and didn't have anything to do with the 'folk up there' as he'd overheard one woman say and then she'd complained about the horrible smell of the scent bearers. One observation he'd made about his people was that they were all vastly different.

Following the unveiling there would be a great feast in the hall. No-one voiced their concern about the amount of food being eaten and wasted so close to a battle but putting on a front was what his father had based his life on.

Villian waited nervously on his ship. They were anchored out of sight, ready for the signal to appear when everyone was in place. He stroked the covered figurehead that would be revealed for the first time.

"I hope this goes as planned, Prince Villian, else we're going to get strung up on the castle walls or made to walk the plank."

He turned to smile at the captain. This ship had been years in the making. When Villian had first suggested it at age fifteen there had been looks. But who says no to a Prince? Especially when his father was the type of man he was. Now, he could see the pride every person had in the ship. It was the best in the fleet. He just hoped his father would approve. He also had the Master Sword select the finest of women to become his warriors. He'd fought hard with his father who said they would be ridiculed for letting women fight. War was a man's world. But Villian didn't agree, and finally he got his way. And what warriors they were.

They were fearless. They trained harder and longer than any of the men Villian had ever fought with. They stood now, proud on the ship. They were warriors born, he knew that. The laughter of his father's personal bodyguards had soon fallen silent after a 'friendly' contest had been arranged years ago, never to be repeated.

"We can always sail away to distant lands." The captain words returned him to his duty.

"That we could, Captain."

"I will have the fleet ready to turnabout at your command, my Prince." At this, the captain bowed, "Prince Villian, may the lady of the sea bring you fortune, and for our own necks, I hope the King bloody likes it."

Villian smiled as the captain left. Hopefully, the show he was about to put on would prove as popular as he'd planned.

He knew when the attack came from their enemies that it would come from the sea as well as the land and if Villian had his way, from the air. It was unlikely they would be defeated at sea, but it would reduce their numbers fighting at the castle. Divide and conquer, that was the goal in war. Weaken the army to the point you create a window of weakness; then strike. He hoped that none of this would be necessary; that he would have the time to bring back the dragons and avoid a pointless war. But a good commander knew to cover all options.

The moment had arrived. The whole delegation was in place. The horn had been sounded. Excitement and expectation was in the air. Prince Villian was at the head of the fleet, the maiden voyage of his new ship. He needed to make an impression no-one would ever forget. They needed to remember him as their courageous Prince, the one trying to save their lands, and very way of life. A Prince who never shied away from a fight, never stopped finding new ways to protect his people. He would need this belief to last after he left, and when he returned victorious. Villian had never felt so sick, the nerves were twitching inside his body, but his ramrod posture belied nothing. To the onlooker he was confident, solid, sure of himself and his place and responsibilities. He needed their belief to power him on. His father was right about one thing; it was all about the show.

The ship came around the headland, fast and sure. The shouts of the sailors were lost on the wind. The horn sounded and the ship started to slow. The captain knew his job, and the weather was smiling down on them, even the wind abated as they came to a stop in the harbour.

The applause was deafening, the captain stood proud, as well he might. The ship had been built for war and to impress and it did both very well. The painted hull told the tale of the great war, when dragons were lost from their world, but the story was forged for the future, a tale of great deeds and the return of the dragons. All seven colours were represented – the dragon families of old.

Villian could see his father, his temporary throne covered in rich cloth, but he couldn't tell if he was happy or not. It was time to reveal the figurehead.

The horns on the ship sounded. The oars were raised in unison and pounded on the decks. His warriors banging the deck with their spears; their cries echoing around the harbour, and bouncing off the castle walls. The crowds cheered. All eyes were on Prince Villian as he stood on the prow; he pulled on the mighty cloth covering the figurehead. The gasps from the crowd were all the confirmation he needed.

The dragonhead, fierce and dominating, its scales painted red as the dragon suggested by Raykan, its mouth opened ready to breathe fire on its enemies. Worked by the best woodcarver in the lands, it looked like it was alive and ready to fly.

Once more the deafening roars and shouts from the crowd spurred him on. He still couldn't read his father, he could see no movement from the throne.

Villian nodded to the captain. It was time.

The captain passed him a torch and Villian touched it to the back of the figurehead. Moments later the flames burst from the mouth of the dragonhead. A man positioned below moved the great bellows. Utter silence was followed by a deafening roar that had never been heard before. This was a show. A show of strength and belief. Villian looked at his father, at that moment he stood with his people, clapping for his son. The harbour crowd erupted into more cheers and screams which could have been heard across the whole of the world. Villian basked in this proud moment and hoped their enemies could hear the cries of their demise.

As Villian strode through the forest, a smile came to his lips thinking of the day. There had been much feasting and drinking and Villian had still felt he needed more sleep when he arrived at Raykan's hut. There had been so much to do, and he'd grown in stature at his father's rare praise. But, no matter how tired he felt, his duties continued into the night.

Walking into Raykan's hut, he soon woke up. There was an air of importance, of something coming. A charge in the air. Magic. It had to be.

He looked at Raykan, who looked like he hadn't slept since Villian had seen him last. Without speaking, Villian went to pour them a strong brew that Raykan always had on the stove.

He set it down and seated himself across from Raykan, waiting for him to speak.

"Do you have everything you need, Son? Are you ready to leave?"

"I am, and yes. This is what we have been working towards these many years."

Raykan nodded, "I heard about your ship." He raised an eyebrow, "I think people will remember Prince Villian for a very long time."

Villian smiled, a blush of pride touching his cheeks, "That's the plan. Your red dragon went down a treat. Now I just need to bring the real dragons back, marry the Lady and live happily ever after; or so the stories go."

"I hope that is the case, my Son, and that I get to see you riding the dragon to glory. Oh, to see a dragon in flight again. To ride a dragon and feel the great power and freedom."

"Again?" Villian exclaimed, mouth open.

"I'm a lot older than I look, my Son. One day, I will tell you my story, but right now it's not impor..."

"Not important! You rode a dragon, Raykan! A dragon. Tell me what it was like. How fast did it go? Did you dive out of the sky? Did it make you feel sick? Did it breathe fire when you were on it?"

Raykan held his hands up to the onslaught of questions.

"Okay, I suppose I'm going to have to answer some of those, or else I will get no sense out of you."

"You have learned many things in the years I have taught you. Your mother was instrumental in setting you on this path. She believed, and she was right to believe in the old stories. To answer you, yes, I once rode a dragon, yes, he did breathe fire and yes it was the best experience of my life. You may now close your mouth, and... no-more questions."

Villian couldn't believe it. His friend and mentor had ridden a dragon, and this was the first time he was hearing about it!

"How old are you?" was all he could manage.

"Impertinent pup, it's rude to ask an elder their age. You of all people should know that."

Villian grinned, "You rode a dragon." He leaned back in his chair, unable to comprehend.

Raykan returned the smile, "Yes I did, Son, and maybe one day, with all the power and luck in the world, one day, you, Prince Villian of Arcus will do the same."

"And possibly learn a bit of magic?" Villian added, the grin still not leaving his face.

"Yes, with a little bit of magic." At this, Raykan closed his eyes and muttered a few words and the roof of the hut disappeared to show the night sky.

Villian stared in wonder. The moon was so large he felt he could reach up and touch it. Thousands of stars blanketed the stunning view. Many a night he had looked upon this sky, but he'd never seen it like this. As he was watching his eye caught a flicker of colour, his eyes locked on as he watched the colours grow: gold, silver, blue, green, red, purple, black swirled in the sky, creating a dance more beautiful than the best fire shows in the castle. The colours weaved and caressed each other until they created a swirling circle of colour.

Too soon, Raykan stopped speaking and the night sky disappeared. It was a few moments before Villian could speak.

"Wow. Can you teach me how to do that?"

"No, it's not the right time for you to learn Magic like that, and besides, that wasn't all my doing. The world has stronger powers than me, young prince."

Villian looked thoughtful, "Why can I not learn? Is it because of the reason the dragons had to leave us? Can you now tell me more about it?"

Raykan eased his body off the chair and went to the stove. He needed a moment to think about how much to share. Even though his injury made moving look painful, Villian marvelled at his ability to move so easily when he must be thousands of years old. He knew that later he wouldn't be able to sleep. Raykan's revelations would spin through his mind.

Setting refilled tankards on the table, Raykan sat down heavily.

"I know I haven't told you as much as I should, and that you've believed in me all this time without hesitation. Believed in the quest, dragons and that magic does exist all to save Arcus and your people. I don't think you realise what a special boy you are. Maybe I shouldn't call you a boy anymore. You're a man and always have been."

Villian blushed under his praise. "It has been my honour. My mother taught me my place in the world and set me on this path. I will not fail her, or you Raykan."

Raykan nodded.

Raykan told him a little about the past. But he didn't want the boy's head filled with things he didn't need to know now. They spent most of the hours going through the plan. Raykan made him repeat every detail to make sure Villian had memorised it, trying to keep it simple so the boy wasn't overwhelmed. Raykan looked across the table at him; his features and temperament the mirror of his mother, with the hair, colour and build of his father. Their hopes and dreams went with him. Far away, he hoped his friend was ready.

In the early hours he'd sent Villian home to get some sleep and prepare himself; tomorrow would be another long day. Raykan needed to make sure he had the opening spell ready.

Shortly after Villian left, there was a knock at the door.

Chapter Fifteen – Suntra

Bluewing flew fast and hard trying to leave his emotions in the past. He understood why, but it didn't make it any easier.

He and his friend had been summoned to the elder mountain – a rare privilege. Pathandon thought that maybe they were going to get in trouble for Bluewing's lack of fire in training yet again. But immediately they knew it was more serious. They didn't usually get called to the council for such minor offences.

All the elders were waiting, Pathandon's grandparents in the middle, with Bluewing's father to the king's side.

'Sons, you two have been chosen to attend this council because the future of our families will lie with you.'

Pathanclaw stared at these two children looking relieved because they'd assumed they were getting in trouble. Could they put so much on their young wings? Did they have a choice?

'As you know, at the last council meeting, the decision was made to attempt to save the humans and find the females lost to us. It has been decided that Pathandon will leave with myself and General Battlewing. Bluewing you will lead the families through once we have secured a safe path.'

Pathanclaw moved onto other matters to give the friends, time to come to terms with their separate futures. Silvarna turned her head, unable to take the crushing emotion when the friends realised they would be parted, and maybe for the last time if it all went wrong. Her heart broke; looking at her husband, she knew he was feeling the same. Not for the first time she wondered how humans dealt with these emotions during their short lives. How did they recover so quickly? She had never been around the humans often when they had lived in peace on Arcus. It was usually only the elder council that met the humans other than on special occasions. She found it hard to communicate with them but was fascinated by their stories.

After years of living together side by side the dragons had become more aware of their emotions. Dragons had thousands of years and humans only a blink of eye. So much to learn and lose in such a short time.

Silvarna felt the gentle touch on her wing from Pathanclaw. She closed her mind, shutting off her emotions and looked back to her grandson and Bluewing.

'Do you have any questions?' the king asked them.

'Why can I not go instead of Pathandon? He is next in line. If anything happens to him, what will our families do?'

Pathanclaw had expected something like this. The General was about to rebuke his son for not using the proper address to the king. But this was a time to talk as friends.

'I respect the great sacrifice you have offered, Bluewing. Your father, this council and your King and Queen are proud of you.'

This had the effect he intended and Bluewing puffed out his already powerful chest. He would be an immense fire-breather and fighter – just like his father.

'We know that not taking you lessens our strength. But we need someone we can trust to look after the Queen and the other families. Blues have always protected us, and long may that continue. Therefore, you must stay. I'm trusting you to look after my wife, Bluewing. I can give no other honour from one dragon to another. I am giving you my very heart. We need Pathandon's magic for this quest to succeed. I know we ask a lot of you. But this is the will of the council. Do you accept?'

Bluewing looked up at his father, knowing he might lose more than just his friend. Pathandon turned to Bluewing and bowed his head; his friend turned and did the same. Their heads touching, a sign of the utmost respect and reserved for family.

'We accept,' Bluewing answered, to his father's pride and profound sadness.

The council finished and before Pathandon could say anything, Bluewing left.

'Leave him, grandson. He will be okay. He just needs time to come to terms with it. It's always harder for the ones left behind. No matter the danger we face.'

Pathandon looked up at his grandfather. He couldn't believe anything in the world could harm this greatest of all dragons. Even in old age he was powerful. How could a mere human harm him, or any of them? A flicker of anger touched his thoughts.

'Don't be angry, Pathandon. Humans can be their own worst enemy. They can be the evilest creatures in the world, but they are also capable of great compassion and kindness. What happened should have been foreseen, but it wasn't. Once we are back on Arcus again, we will not make the same mistakes of the past. It is time to right the wrongs. You know the old stories.'

'I know, grandsire. Forgive my anger. I'm going to find Bluewing now before he does something he will regret.'

He nodded and allowed him to go after his friend. They needed to enjoy the time they had left together, as did he. He went to seek Silvarna.

Chapter Sixteen – Luminosa

Pol and Star stared at the Suckers. Pol made to move forward, and Star pulled them back. Dragon had found her and was making a low crying noise. He must have sensed her distress.

"Hush, Dragon," Star said, more harshly than she meant to, but they couldn't be discovered. She stroked Dragon's head to show she wasn't angry.

Star's gaze followed the dry arid sands that went on as far as the eye could see. The scorching sun was beating down. So, unlike the lush green of the forest. It was a barren wasteland barring the heart-breaking sight before them. Her eyes returned to the giant chains that were secured to the ground, each ring the height of a human adult. Tears welled in her eyes as her gaze rested on the end of the chain, a dragon. Bigger than anything Star had ever seen. A huge ugly metal contraption covered the dragon's head. It made her feel sick. They looked as if they were only given enough food to keep them alive. The metal muzzle wouldn't allow for much food to pass, and despite their great size they looked diminished.

Looking past the Suckers... No! Dragons, she berated herself. Never would she call them Suckers again; she looked at the heat shimmering off the dry hot ground. The heat must be unbearable, it was hotter than in the centre of the camp. If any child had tried to leave, they wouldn't get far across that land. Again, the contrast between the beautiful lush forest full of life with the vision of the death that lay ahead made her shiver. If they had to escape the camp to that, she knew they would all be lost.

Dragon whined again. She stroked her head thinking it was funny that Dragon reacted like that. Were all dragons made from magic and not born? Did dragons come from human magic? Her head hurt thinking about it.

Star couldn't help but stare at these poor creatures, although the memory of what she'd seen would live with her forever. The times they had joked about the 'Suckers', the giant slugs, Triana making them scary for the newbies and Star and Thanan making jokes to drive the fear from the children. Never could they have imagined this. She thought even Triana would feel bad; well, maybe not.

'Why don't they do something? Try to get away? Why don't they burn the Masters?' she said to Pol.

One of the dragons lifted its giant head, and she could see it tilt in their direction. She grabbed Pol and they bent down behind a tree to make sure they wouldn't be spotted by the guards. Star was sure it was looking at them. She hoped it wouldn't give them away. Very slowly it lowered its head. Star could swear it looked like it had bowed its great head to them before it rested on the ground.

A group of guards wandered up and down the line of dragons. They didn't seem scared of their captives. They were not Masters, only normal men. Did they know about the children in camp? How come they had stayed and not left at thirteen? Star still couldn't believe the size of the dragons! Would her Dragon grow up to be that big? Who were these guards? They didn't dress in the hooded cloaks. Were these the Masters without the cloaks? Is this all they were? They dressed in no more than rags, like the children in the camp. Whilst they were watching one of them took out a whip and used it on a dragon. All the others laughed. The dragon would barely feel it though their thick scales, but clearly it amused these evil people.

She looked at Pol, realising they hadn't answered her earlier question. Pol had been still throughout.

At the sight of the whip, Pol stood up and Star took a step back. Pol's eyes had turned black. She'd never seen her friend like this. Normally quiet and small, they looked more dangerous than any Master ever had. If they weren't careful, they would be caught. They had to get away, even more so now they had seen this. They had even more reason to leave and return one day with help to free not only the children but the dragons as well. They couldn't risk being caught now, not when they were so close to leaving together.

Gently, Star touched her friend's arm, *'Pol. Are you okay? We must leave. This is too dangerous. Please, we must get back.'*

At first, she didn't think Pol was going to respond. Star could feel a vibration running through Pol's body.

'Pol. It's okay. We will come back one day and stop this. We cannot do it now. We need more help. But we will come back. I promise.'

Pol turned to her, tears streaming down their face. Their now orange eyes were so sorrowful, Star could barely look at them; it made her heart ache. Star grabbed Pol and hugged them tight, her tall body enveloping her friend's small frame. Trying to take away the pain, she stroked Pol's short hair and murmured soothing words like a mother would.

'I promise we will come back and save them Pol. I promise. I will not rest until we come back and save them and make the Masters pay. They will pay for this, Pol. They will.'

Dragon landed on Pol's shoulder and rubbed her face gently against them. Pol's hand came up and stoked Dragon's face and then Pol placed both hands on Star's face.

'One day, I will kill them all.'

Star felt a chill run through her body as Pol turned away and walked back into the forest, her now purple eyes blazing.

Chapter Seventeen – Arcus

Villian had spent years preparing for this day, and now he didn't know what to do with himself. His leather backpack was filled with everything he thought he might need. His sword had been sharpened and cleaned; his daggers had been given the same treatment. The castle seamstress had outdone herself; the hidden pockets were perfect in his new trousers and jacket. His blankets were made from the lightest material possible.

He'd chosen tan coloured, understated clothing, although he would have liked to show off to the people as he left, riding a white horse, with his banners flowing in the wind, trumpets blaring, and his family sigil of the Red Dragon draped on his steed. Raykan had sighed and told him to stop being so childish. That had stung. Of course he knew that he needed to leave quietly. If he succeeded though, maybe this would be his welcome return. He'd had the sigil sewn into the inside of his tunic – close to his heart.

Everything was ready, and there was nothing else for him to do other than to perform his last duty before he left. It was the eve of the Festival of Time, and by tomorrow night he would be leaving. But, right now he was still Prince Villian, future King of Arcus. Tonight, he would be betrothed to Lady Cartina, in the hope that her family would join them and fight the oncoming army. If he wasn't intending to leave, there was no chance Villian would have agreed. But, what did it matter to him whom his father betrothed him to now? After he went missing tonight, the search would reveal a letter which he'd left with a book to be returned to the Keeper – he was sure that letter would be given to his father and he would realise his son was trying to save the world. He would be proud. Especially after the successful display with the ship. His father would know the kingdom would be safe in his hands.

His aides came in to dress him in his finery. Back straight, he walked tall into the hall, aware as every eye tracked his movement. He nodded as required. Behaved as a prince. Many noblemen were eager to curry favour with their future king. They had heard the rumours about his father's failing health in the last few weeks. If the war didn't finish him off, that cough would.

Even after all these years Villian couldn't help but be impressed by the hall. If anyone needed any evidence that dragons existed, they need look no further. Why would humans need to build a room so large? The huge glass dome roof worked on humongous sized chains the size of wagon wheels. They hadn't been opened in hundreds of years and the metal workings had grown rusty. Villian had argued on many occasions, demanding how mere humans could have opened them. And why would anyone build a roof that could open if they couldn't fly? Surely it was for the dragons to enter the throne room as equals, friends? His questions had fallen on disbelieving ears.

As he took his place next to his stepmother and father, he took a deep breath, ready to do his unwilling duty.

She was beautiful. Villian's mind went blank, and he found himself speechless. Lady Cartina was beautiful. A year younger than him, at sixteen she was a queen in waiting. Her family had clearly spent a lot of coins on her dress. Magnificent in gold and red, she opened her arms wide as she walked down the central aisle, the pattern of her dress had been created to look like dragon wings. The audience gasped at the show and splendour. Her father, mother and a large procession followed behind. Her face was so pale compared to his, she looked like she was made from the alabaster they mined in the mountains, like the statue of his mother.

"My King, Queen, Prince of Arcus, and Lord and Ladies of Arcus, I present to you my daughter, Lady Cartina, that she may unite with your most honourable son, Prince Villian, and join our houses in the defence of our lands." Her father bowed low, his hand letting go of Lady Cartina as she moved forward to stand in front of the thrones.

It took a while for the deafening noise of support to settle down. The king gave him his dues: her father knew how to work a crowd. With a wave of his hand the noise settled, and he welcomed his esteemed visitors to even more noise. The feasting began.

Villian had been seated next to Lady Cartina throughout, but they had barely exchanged a few words. Villian, for all his upbringing, didn't know what to say. When the music started, they got up first, as was expected, and they shyly danced around each other. Villian was in awe of her beauty. He caught a glance between Lady Cartina, and her father and she paled – if that were possible. He realised her father was not happy because they were not engaging to his satisfaction.

He straightened his back. He was a king's son after all, a man about to embark on a secret quest no less. If he couldn't even talk to a beautiful girl, how would he manage in another time – another world?

"Lady Cartina. Please forgive my manners, I'm so in awe of your beauty that you have rendered me speechless."

Cartina blushed a deep red, adding much needed colour to her face. Good, Villian thought, better than the paleness her father had impressed on her.

"Thank you, Prince Villian. I was beginning to think I didn't please you."

"Looks aren't everything. A man I'm very friendly with is hideous but he still pleases me."

She looked shocked.

"Wait, sorry. Not that I think you're hideous. Sorry. Wait, can we start again?"

She laughed, a beautiful, lady-like laugh, gentle as the breeze.

What was happening to him? They moved back to their seats as others moved to dance.

"You're forgiven, Prince Villian. Since we're betrothed to spend the rest of our lives together, I should think it would be better that we liked each other."

It was Villian's turn to blush. He took a large drink from his flagon and started to choke. Lady Cartina patted him helpfully on the back.

"Please don't die. The alternative is for me to marry someone who is at least eighty. I doubt he would manage the wedding night."

Villian was so shocked he burst out laughing and Lady Cartina joined in. Villian noticed their fathers looking happier. Obviously, everything was going to their plan. It annoyed him to think someone was ruling his life, but already he felt comfortable with this young girl whom he would soon be leaving. Would they make her wait or wed her to the other man? Villian felt an unexpected wave of jealously wash over him. He'd only known this girl a matter of hours, but already he felt somehow their lives had joined along the same path.

"Shall we go for a walk?"

"That would be nice, my Prince."

He liked the way she said that. A plan was forming in his mind. He couldn't have this young girl left bereft, but he had a quest to attend to. What would a Prince of old have done?

Her maids rose and he signalled for them to remain seated. They looked to Lady Cartina's father and he gave a slight nod.

Villian held out his arm and Cartina slipped her arm through his. A perfect fit. He'd read about love at first sight but thought that was just in fairy tales and girls' dreams. To happen to him, now, tonight, of all nights. Maybe it was the excitement of leaving.

The moon in the sky was full, and he wished he could show her the lights as Raykan had showed him; how impressed she would be. Tomorrow night the portal would be open, and he would have to leave. They walked arm in arm through the gardens, silence already comfortable between them.

"Do you feel the same as me?" Cartina said shyly, then added, "I feel like I've known you all my life. How silly. I came here ready to hate my life, betrothed to someone I'd never met. Sorry, I've gotten into trouble all my life for speaking without thinking. I'm not sure that I'm the right person to marry off to the most powerful family on Arcus. They should have sent my sister."

Villian turned to look at this girl he'd only just met. "I'm glad they sent you." He bent forward and kissed her hand. "I need to tell you something, Lady Cartina. Something important, a secret that cannot be shared with anyone. Can I trust you?"

Fool, Villian could hear Raykan's voice in his head. Telling a stranger your secret after so short a time. But he hadn't got where he was without being able to know someone's character, and he knew already he could trust his future wife with his life.

"You can trust me, Prince Villian. On my honour, I swear it."

"Please, just call me Villian." He took a deep breath, and told her he was going on an adventure; even though he felt he could trust her he didn't want to place her in danger. She need only know he would be leaving, but not where he was going; only that he would return to save them all.

Lady Cartina was quiet for a while, and then she nodded.

"My hope beyond you returning safely is that you do not find me married to that eighty-year-old, grumpy nobleman." This was said with a tremor in her voice.

"I know a way we can avoid that."

Without further thought, Villian took her arm and strode through the gardens and back into the feasting room. Signalling a guard to quieten the room, he announced his engagement to Lady Cartina by bending down on one knee and offering her his hand. The room erupted.

"Now then," he whispered as he stood up, "that is settled. All you need do is wait."

Chapter Eighteen - Suntra

Pathanclaw and Pathandon left the mountain, Battlewing had been waiting outside to escort them back. Even here, where they had no natural enemy, the General would not break protocol. A Blue must be at their side.

They had flown all day and late into the evening to reach their destination. They were greeted by one of the Black dragons; the Guardians of the gems. Pathandon didn't know their names. It was never shared amongst these secretive dragons. For them, to give a name, was to identify, to impress an order of assumption, to create a link, a knowledge that could somehow be used. They were the Guardians. They had one role in life and that was to protect the gems. They were the most important of all dragons. They nurtured the very essence of how dragons used magic.

Pathanclaw had only been to the cave once when they'd arrived on Suntra and everything was in chaos. The loss of the dragons left behind to die, and the ones lost along the way were felt keenly by all. The guardian of the gems had disappeared the first night and none had questioned it; it was their way. Pathanclaw had awoken one evening many years after they had settled on their new world and had been summoned to the mountain.

Pathandon was nervous, it was an unusual feeling for a dragon. He felt the great weight of responsibility. He and Bluewing speculated all day about what it meant to be summoned to the lair of the Guardians. They were mysterious, and most had never seen a Guardian until they had joined the battle practice. It had taken even the great General time to settle them all when they had showed up to practise the battle flight. It wasn't expected, and after the excitement, a feeling of unease settled. Somehow, everything felt more serious.

They followed the Black dragon deep into the cave, the large hole narrowing to the point where it was a struggle for Pathanclaw to get through. The Black dragons were so much smaller, but Pathandon could feel their power, even though they were not as graceful on the ground as they were in the air. Eventually the tunnel opened into a cave that made them pause before entering. Pathanclaw had of course been in a gem cave before but it was his grandson's first time here.

All the colours were represented here. It was a discussion he'd had with humans over the years. Humans believed gems were made from what they call minerals, and while this might be so on some planets, here, as on Arcus, they were created by dragons. This is where all dragons went to die when their time came. Pathanclaw hoped their last resting place should be so fortunate. The gems' power, a dragon's power and so the circle is forever flowing. Dragons are born, they use the power of the gems and they go back to power others. It is considered an honour to do the final flight. Even though they are parted from the world, the dead live on forever.

Pathanclaw wanted his grandson to see it. To feel it. To know what they were fighting for. To know his responsibility and his part to play in the history of the dragons. In the history of everything. The only time a dragon would normally be given this honour would be their last ever journey. This was the start of Pathandon's journey in life, the start of a big adventure which would hopefully end in peace for them all. Pathanclaw felt ready to make this last flight, hoped that he and Silvarna would be able to do this together when the end came.

Bluewing had ordered Pathandon to tell him everything about it when he returned. To get to see the last resting place of the dragons was only the right of the king, because once a dragon entered there was normally no return journey to tell anyone. But Pathandon knew he wouldn't be able to share any of this with his friend. It wouldn't be respectful to the countless thousands of dragons that had created this place. Pathandon marvelled at the sheer size of it. How many dragons had died to create this seemingly endless cave glittering with all the colours of the dragons? He could also see why such mystery surrounded the Black dragons. They were the link between the living and the dead. They were the channel to the power of the Magic that dragons possessed.

Pathandon was thoughtful on the way back. They had talked for many hours with the Guardians of the gems. If their first quest were successful, they would need to bring all the dragons through and leave this world. This would mean that a few would need to be left behind to give them the link to the power. The chance of ever joining them on Arcus was unlikely and this was a decision even a King could not make for another. The Guardians were non-plussed by the request. By nature, they lived longer than any other dragon and craved solitude.

Matters settled; they'd taken their leave. It had been agreed that two would remain and two would leave to return to Arcus. If they were successful, they would be the last ever living dragons the Guardians of the gems would see. Eventually, with no new dragons the gems would diminish and theirs would be the last left. Maybe they would be found, one day, at another moment in time if Suntra was ever inhabited again.

Chapter Nineteen – Luminosa

Thanan fidgeted, trying to get comfortable. Normally he settled into his elevated position with ease, but today his mind couldn't settle, which meant his body didn't allow the magic to do its work. He'd found this before: he felt uncomfortable in his own skin when the magic didn't work cohesively. After his free morning he'd decided to visit Tobias again.

"Will you please focus your mind, Thanan?" Tobias said firmly, but with a hint of sympathy. After all, his friend knew why he was so unsettled.

"Sorry. I know I need to concentrate, and I have so much to learn before I leave. But I'm scared of what will happen. I'm scared of staying and scared of going."

Only here would Thanan be so honest. Only here, could he share his fears and emotions without judgement or scorn. He thought about what Triana would say if she knew his true thoughts and feelings.

"You're doing it again."

"Sorry," Thanan said, and mentally made his body relax and the magic and calm washed over him.

"Finally. Now tell me again your plans."

They had gone over and over it many times, tweaking it and trying to think of every possibility. They were nearly there. The Festival of Time was nearly upon them. He hoped they were ready. They had to be ready. As always, these sessions were a source of great hope and sadness: the hope that he and his friends could escape, and the sadness that he would be leaving his friend and mentor. Once they'd left, he doubted they would ever meet again.

Hours later and the plans were laid more firmly into his mind. Thanan disconnected and floated back to the ground; his long legs landed in a puddle of water because he wasn't paying attention. The damp cave never dried out and he'd got used to the smell of the place over time, warming to the dank musty smell that lingered on his clothes. It reminded him of Tobias. It was also never truly light in the cave. The only light coming from the many worms that hung from the roof, all emitting different colours, creating tricks of the light when the colours merged. Sometimes it was just infinite blackness.

"Idiot," came the voice behind him.

Thanan didn't need to look to know who it was. His arch enemy, Triana.

"Get lost, Triana."

"If there is anyone likely to get lost it would be you Thanan." Her haughty voice annoyed him. She'd said her parents had volunteered for her to come to camp due to her natural magical ability. Thanan had thought that was a silly thing to say. Who would want to be sent away from their parents to a camp, instead of being at home? That's why everyone treated her like the queen of the camp, hangers-on desperate for her attention, hopeful that she might have some influence. Fat chance. Thanan had met her sort before. They disappeared like all the rest. And, he didn't think she remembered her past any better than any of the children. She was very vague when asked to share specifics.

He walked out to sniggers. Pol appeared at his side, as they did. In the early days, it used to make him jump, but now he was used to it. His eyes took a few moments to adjust to the light outside, the purple sky turning to black, signalling it was time to eat. The sessions with Tobias had made him hungry as usual. He saw Pol peer over their shoulder and give Triana a look. Thanan shivered, he wouldn't want that look trained on him. He touched Pol's arm and said, "She's not worth it, Pol."

He knew what they were thinking. Pol would do anything to protect him and Star, but they were so close to leaving they couldn't let anyone know that Pol could perform magic whenever they wanted.

It wasn't like Pol to react so angrily to Triana, since they were all used to her behaviour by now. Pol smiled at him and in his mind he could see exactly what they'd intended to do; Triana tripped and fell, face first into a dirty hole in the cave's entrance, which included the green rain from earlier in the day. Standing up, dripping wet and her face dyed green, even her steadfast bully friends couldn't help but laugh.

Thanan fell about laughing at a scene only they could see, although Thanan noticed the smile didn't reach Pol's eyes. Something was wrong. As they moved away from the group, Triana and her friends looked on, secretly wishing they had such good friends.

"She's acting like dragon dung. Nothing new there?" Star caught up with them as they entered the clearing. Star always looked like she was ready for a fight. She had an aggressive walk, and it would often make Triana think twice when they were together as a group, their past encounters fresh in both their minds. To be fair, Thanan wouldn't want to take Star on. Her stature matched her attitude. She looked different from the confidence of the morning though, she looked like she'd aged since breakfast.

"What's wrong?" Thanan asked.

Star looked at Pol, "We need to tell you something, Thanan. But let's get some food and sit down, although I'm not sure I can eat."

They picked their meal from the bush and settled down; not that any of them enjoyed it once Star had told her story.

Thanan felt sick. Dragons; on Luminosa. The 'Suckers' were dragons! How could that be? Tobias had told him in one world the humans and dragons lived together in harmony – that couldn't be true, or else why would the humans not rescue the dragons?

'I don't think they have a choice, Thanan. You should have seen them chained up. It was awful.'

An unusual silence descended on the trio of friends; Thanan imaging – Pol and Star not having to.

'Do you think we need to stay and help them?' Star asked.

'No,' Pol answered, 'we need to leave before you and Thanan are taken.'

Star was surprised at Pol's quick response and the long answer. From the look on Pol's face at the time they could have taken down the whole of the camp and freed them without the need of help. Not for the first time Star wondered about Pol's powers and what they truly were. Looking up, Star saw Pol looking at her, a sadness that broke Star's heart rested on her friend.

'Pol is right, Star. I feel the same as you. To think there have been dragons here all this time and we didn't know, and they are being kept like slaves and prisoners just like us. But, we must get away from this place before your name day. Then we will work out how we can come back and save them.'

The thought of getting out of this place was hard enough. To think of coming back and saving the dragons, how could they do it? They were only children. Yes, they had the power to do magic. But still, against the Masters they would need more than just the three of them. It seemed impossible. He knew their magic wouldn't be enough.

They looked down as Pol joined their hands with their friends. In their minds they could see a huge landscape. Many mountains, higher than anything here. Animals running across the plains, great deserts and seas. They were swooping higher and faster. The image shifted to the left and they saw a blue dragon gliding in the sky; graceful, fast, menacing, a great ball of flame shot out into the sky. On the other side a red dragon, strong and graceful. The image faded and silence once again descended on the group.

Thanan looked at Star and saw a stupid grin that he knew was mirrored in his own face.

'Is that real, Pol?'

Pol nodded but would say no more, no matter how many questions they asked. It was very frustrating, but that was Pol.

Soon their thoughts went back to more imminent issues. Thoughts of dragons brought conflicting feelings.

'Okay, so I think we have everything. We've got the light. All our kit, and the plan. Before midnight in two days' time, Star, you will gather everything, and, Pol, you grab some food for the journey.'

Star and Pol nodded, Star unable to speak due to the large bite of food she'd taken. The juice leaked out the side of her mouth, and the pips fell down her chin. Thanan sighed and Pol smiled, happy that Star's appetite had come back, and a smile had returned to his friends' faces. The strain of the day was easing just a little.

"Pol, you need to make sure that we get the right Pol for the job that night. We need to take it seriously. We cannot risk anything going wrong."

Pol and Star smirked at each other, and Thanan rolled his eyes. One look at him and Pol nodded, serious again, eye colour changed in an instant.

'What about you, he-that-knows-everything? What exactly will you be doing?" Star said.

"I have to be prepared with the alternative plan in case this goes wrong and we cannot leave through the portal. Tobias has told me about a secret network of caves where we could hide until we figure out what to do next. It's not much, and I really don't know what we are going to do, but we cannot just give up if this goes wrong."

"How does he know it's there? Can we go and have a look at the caves? Where are the secret caves and why didn't we already know about them?" Star said. Her flurry of questions coming thick and fast as was her way.

"Tobias knows everything. Of course, he knows where it is. I just need to figure out how we will survive if we end up in them!"

"Maybe we need a diversion?" Star said, with that glint which Thanan didn't like. She added excitedly, *"Yes, since it won't matter as we will be out of here anyway!"*

Pol clapped their hands delightedly and they all smiled. Pol having changed back at Star's encouragement no doubt.

"I don't want to know," Thanan said. He would only worry if he knew what she was planning.

Star was silent which worried Thanan. Clearly, she was planning an event to end all events. This was exactly her sort of thing. Maximum chaos and mischief. Dragon swooped and dived; an extension of how she was feeling. Eventually she settled clumsily on Star's shoulder. Thanan didn't think that could happen for much longer, Dragon certainly was growing.

"Have you got a name for her yet?" Thanan asked.

"No, nothing seems to fit her right. I'm waiting for inspiration. Until then I'm just going to keep calling her Dragon."

"Your imagination is second to none."

Star nudged him, almost knocking him off the stump. Dragon opened her mouth and screamed in Thanan's direction, a small puff of smoke surrounded his face and he started coughing. Through his spluttering, Thanan could hear his friend's laughter. He didn't mind, it was cool that Star's dragon was growing up. At least it hadn't been a ball of fire. It seemed Dragon was learning how to control her fire. It would be useful. They couldn't imagine now how important Dragon would be.

Chapter Twenty – Arcus

What a night. Villian lay on his bed, his head resting on his muscly arms, staring at the ceiling. His emotions were all over the place. Why had it happened tonight? Why had he met Lady Cartina tonight, of all nights. His thoughts should be about his quest, but all he could think of was her long red hair, her bright brown eyes and beautiful mouth. Then there was Raykan and his revelations. He knew he needed sleep tonight, but he thought it would be impossible. He only had a few hours before he needed to get up and start what would be anything but a normal day. Trying to put the evening to the back of his mind, he turned on his side and calming his racing mind he fell quickly into an exhausted sleep.

A few hours later he awoke feeling more refreshed than he should after so little sleep. He climbed off the bed and went to his desk, quickly penning a letter to Lady Cartina, saying all the things he would say if he were staying. He would ask Raykan to give her the letter. He tucked it into his tunic as he dressed.

The feast had long finished as he made his way out of his room. There was no point in trying to be quiet. Guards were posted all around the castle. They were used to him wandering in the early morning hours, training with his Master Sword, so it came as no surprise when he made his way through the castle. There were greetings of congratulations from some of the soldiers he knew well, the ones he trusted not to pass on his whereabouts to his father or his aide.

This was his favourite time of day; it was busy, but people were quietly going about their business as castles never slept. There was constant movement and noise. Fires being attended to; the smell of the bread being prepared for the break of the fast; horses being groomed in the stables. He made his way to the kitchens and picked up a large pie and bread, much to the delight of the cook. He already had some cured meat in his pack but a little for the road wouldn't harm.

As he made his way through the courtyard a flash of colour caught his eye. The figure came out of the shadows. It was his betrothed. He went quickly over to her and taking her hand, found a room by the side of the stable where they could hide. He closed the door quietly, sure, they wouldn't have been seen.

"What are doing up at this time and without your maids? Your father will have you locked up." He couldn't hide the matching smile. He was beyond delighted to see her before he left.

"I told you last night, my father should have brought my sister. I tend to have a mind of my own, and I have snuck away from my maids on many occasions over the years. I'm rather an expert at it."

His smile widened, "Another thing we have in common. I can see that on my return I will have my hands full."

A sadness passed over her face and he reached up and gently smoothed out her frown.

"Don't be sad. I will be back, and peace again will reign."

"How can you be so sure? Why are you going alone and not taking guards with you?"

"Where I'm going, I cannot take anyone with me. I must go alone. I'm sorry, but I cannot tell you anymore. It's for your own safety."

"But that only makes me worry more."

"I don't want you to worry. I don't want to remember you looking sad. I want to remember your beautiful smile so it will call me home."

Villian wondered where all this came from. He had gone from no interest in girls, to falling in love overnight. Could this be real love, so quickly? He could only imagine what Ironhand would say.

Cartina smiled, trying to take the sadness from her eyes. "I wanted to give you a gift to remember me by."

His betrothed reached down and lifted his hand. With shaking fingers she opened his hand and reached into her pocket. She placed a ring into his palm.

"It was my grandfathers. My father was unhappy that he never had any sons. My grandfather and I were very close before he died, and he gave me this ring. See, it's really two rings made as if one. He told me to give half to the man I knew would look after me, respect my decisions and forgive my stubbornness." Her voice carried so much emotion that it broke at the last, and tears fell down her porcelain face.

Villian reached up with his other hand and wiped them away. "Your grandfather was a wise man and if he were here, I'm sure he would be proud of your choice. Although we might have to see how my forgiveness of your stubbornness goes."

Cartina laughed as he intended. She took one of the rings out of her hand and fitted it onto his left-hand forefinger. It fitted perfectly. He in turn placed one on hers. He marvelled that the ring fitted so perfectly. How could that be? Her fingers were so delicate and small. Not like his. He would have to ask Raykan about this. Could there be magic involved?

"I promise I will never take it off until I return, and we are wed. I wish I had something for you."

"It doesn't matter. I will remain here in the castle until you return, and traces of you are everywhere. I will walk where you have walked. I will even sail on your ship and think of you. I will command your warrior army. Although they are a little scary!"

He laughed. He could picture this delicate girl commanding his fierce warriors.

Villian remembered the letter, "Wait, I do have this." Reaching into his tunic, he took out the letter. He had sealed it with his royal seal, the red dragon.

Cartina took the letter and held it to her heart. "I will memorise your words and think of you until you return."

Villian reached over and kissed her forehead before turning to leave.

"Go back to your quarters now before you are missed. My first command as your betrothed."

There was mischief in her eyes as she matched his glare. "As you command my lord." She curtsied, then quickly reached up and kissed him on the cheek, before running off towards the kitchen and not in the direction of her quarters.

Villian laughed quietly, thinking he had met his match. With happiness and sadness in his heart, he left his betrothed and made his way to see his friends for the last time before he turned his attention to his future. Raykan would be waiting.

He hid his backpack in his secret hiding place ready for later and made his way for his morning training with the Master Sword. As he walked through the large stone archway he just managed to dodge and roll out of the way before the wooden practice sword smashed into the wall.

He heard a chuckle from his left. Morbark liked to spring these surprises on him, keep him on his toes, although Villian wondered if one day it would all go terribly wrong and Morbark would be left explaining why he'd cut off the head of the king's only son!

Villian was on his feet in a moment and one of the other trainers threw him a practice sword. Looking around the clearing he said, "Well this isn't fair. Five against one?" He didn't have chance to say anything further as they all attacked.

Villian's legs and arms were burning when they'd finished. Barring a few bruises, the others had come away a lot worse. They enjoyed it as much as him and everyone left with a grin, followed by a grimace. They would all be sore in the morning.

"Well done, my Prince. You fought well today. You will not need my services soon." Morbark bowed low.

Villian was encouraged by the praise. He'd held a sword from such a young age and couldn't remember a time without one.

"Thank you. I had a good teacher."

Villian returned the bow and handed the wooden sword back. To the shock of the Master Sword he embraced his teacher, knowing it would be a long time before he saw him again, hoping that he could bring back the help they needed before the fighting started. Villian knew Morbark would be first to battle if it came to it. He was fearless, and renowned for his ruthlessness. It was in stark contrast to his calm demeanour, in the summer games it was rare for him to lose.

Morbark returned his embrace and without another word Villian left to head to the hall for more food. Morbark looked at the departing prince, questions and decisions forming quickly in his experienced mind. He strode away from the training room with purpose.

After lunch Villian left to seek out Ironhand. Lady Cartina and her family had been present at lunch, but as was the custom they would be kept separate until the wedding day. Courting over. Decision made. The upcoming war had put these plans into motion. Normally they would get to know each other for months before the formal announcement would be made. He knew his father had been overjoyed at his decision last night; with the enemy approaching they didn't have time for such things, but they needed the power and army Cartina's family afforded. They needed to be bonded by more than just promises.

Villian stopped to talk to a few of the castle inhabitants before heading to the smithy. The noise reached his ears before the sight of Ironhand's home. Since he'd seen the dragon book, he'd been keen to interrogate the smith some more. He was certain Ironhand knew more than he had let on, and if Raykan was impressed someone knew something about the book, Villian wanted to know more. It wasn't often he got the upper hand on his friend in the woods. He would have to play it carefully though, Ironhand was stubborn as a mule when pressed.

Ironhand's apprentice was looking frantic as his master barked out his orders and disapproval. Villian wouldn't have liked to have been his student. He'd learned a lot from his friend, but teaching a friend and a prince was different. This boy would grow up to be as good as Ironhand if he continued. Already Villian could see the boy's muscular form changing. He would be enormous at the end of his training and he wasn't sure that Ironhand would be able to control him. Villian would pay to see that day of reckoning.

"Why if it isn't the newly betrothed Prince. Love at first sight my boy? I expected better from you." Ironhand roared with laughter and Villian was grateful for the excuse of the furnace warming his cheeks.

"News travels fast."

"Are you surprised? Proposing on the first night? Hours after meeting the Lady. What were you thinking? Too much of that royal mead running through your blood, I will wager. Been reading those history books of Princes of old."

Villian felt a little annoyed. Did people see this as a weakness in him? Not to wait the normal period before announcing the engagement. Did they think him stupid?

"Calm down, my Prince. I'm only joking. Every girl in the castle has been swooning since they heard. You might have made a few enemies of the men, mind you. They have even more to live up to now."

Villian relaxed. His mother always told him not to worry about what others thought. To listen yes, to change if needed; but not to take harmless comments and let them eat away at him.

"I've come for my chains." Villian held out his wrists.

This earned another roar of laughter from his friend. The boy sagged with relief, as if he thought Prince Villian would have them all beheaded.

"Come then. I could eat a whole pig. Let's eat. Boy, those swords better be done when I get back or else I will string you up and roast you over the fire."

They made their way out of the back of the smithy and to the ale house.

"In a few years' time I think he will be too big for you to boss around. He's going to be a hulk of a man."

"I know. Why do you think I'm working him hard? If he's terrified of me, he will think twice about taking me on."

Villian laughed, knowing that it was all a front. Ironhand's bark was worse than his bite, but not everyone realised that.

Settled in their familiar spot in the back of the inn, Ironhand tucked into his food, and despite his large breakfast, Villian was ravenous due to the sword training. He stretched out his long legs trying to take the ache out of them. The sword fight had been brutal.

"So," Ironhand said between mouthfuls, "what brings you here again today? I have a feeling you have something to tell me."

"I'm leaving tonight. I cannot tell you any more than that. If I didn't trust you, I wouldn't be mentioning it. I'm also telling you this so that you understand that I don't have time to wait for your answer."

Villian paused to take a drink, Ironhand had stopped eating.

"Spit it out then, my Prince."

"I need to know everything you know about the book and the precious stones."

His giant friend finished his food, took a drink of his mead, then wiped his mouth.

"You've been talking to Raykan again haven't you? Filling you with magic tales and great deeds."

Villian was shocked. He didn't think anyone knew about him and Raykan. He suddenly felt worried, his stomach churned. How many other people knew? Had he not been as careful as he thought? How had Ironhand found out? Was he a threat to his quest?

"Don't worry, my Prince. I would forfeit my life before I broke my word and friendship with you."

Villian nodded, feeling slightly guilty for even questioning his friend, even if he had not voiced it. He had been nothing but a loyal friend to him all his life.

"Sorry, Ironhand. Is reading minds one of your skills as well?"

The giant grinned. "I have many skills, Prince Villian. As to your questions about the book and stones, there is little I can add that will be of any use to you. I told you everything that I knew would help you."

"There must be something you can tell me? About the metal, or what's inside. Raykan took it off me and I haven't even seen past the first page."

"He will have squirrelled that away on one of his shelves – you will never see that again. Should have looked while you had the chance."

This shocked him again. Clearly Ironhand, had been to Raykan's hut.

"I know that now. Are you sure there is nothing else you can tell me? It seems you and Raykan are friends, maybe he has told you something?"

Ironhand was silent for a few minutes.

"You're going on a journey, that much I know. Anything else, is not for me to say. If I could tell you anything that would help you it would have been said already."

Frustrated, Villian asked, "Do you know where I am going?"

Ironhand didn't answer at first. Then he looked directly at him and a large grin changed the shape of his face.

"Straight back to the smithy to try on your shackles young Prince." At this he adopted his typical roar. Villian heard a woman scream in the next room. His laughter bellowed through the streets and Villian soon joined in. This man was as immovable in body as he was in mind.

After saying goodbye and feeling like Ironhand had crushed every bone in his body, he headed to the library. He wished he could take his friend with him; he would be a useful bodyguard. It was the last goodbye and the one he wasn't sure he should do or how he would do it.

Marching down the long corridors he felt the melancholy of the day. It would be the last time he would see his home for how long, he didn't know. He felt the weight of his quest. He'd never lacked confidence in his life; never doubted his belief in what he had to do. Despite his young age he had been brought up differently to everyone else, his mother the driving force.

The weight of doubt seemed to hang off him, getting heavier and heavier as he made his way to the library. He was just a young boy, why did he think he could save Arcus? They had a whole army with decades of experience; how was he better than them? He had a plan but so many other things relied on chance and hope. Raykan had told him all would be well, but what if he arrived and the path wasn't clear. What would he do? Should he give up and put his energy into war and winning the battle from here? Could he truly succeed?

"YES," he shouted to the corridor. His voice vibrated off the walls getting louder and louder as it echoed around him.

The weight lifted, and Villian felt himself again. What had just happened?

Opening the large wooden library doors. He entered the dusty smelling library.

"Shhhh."

Villian jumped at the voice next to him. He hadn't even seen the Keeper of the Books when he scanned the room.

He was sure he saw a smile as the Keeper moved to his desk. Sitting down, he picked up his quill. Villian followed him and when he was seated, he suddenly felt nervous. His emotions were not behaving as they should today.

The Keeper didn't look up as he opened a book and started to write, ignoring Prince Villian's presence as usual. Villian coughed and the Keeper sighed and put his quill down, arching a brow to invite conversation.

"Erm, I won't be able to attend my lessons for a while. I have urgent business, but I will... erm... come back when I'm... erm back."

Villian knew he sounded like an idiot. The Keeper must think he'd never read any of the books he'd given him over the years. Never learnt the beautiful language of words. That his teachings here had been wasted.

The Keeper glared at him, nodded, picked up his quill and went back to his scribing.

Villian waited a few moments and then realised he had been dismissed. After one last look around, he focused on the desk he'd spent many hours studying at and trying to stay quiet. He'd scratched his name into it when he was a young child. He ran his fingers across the grooves, sealing the memory.

He opened the door and after passing through it he said, "Goodbye." He wasn't sure if it was to the Keeper, the room or his old life. As he closed the door, he thought he heard a reply.

Goodbyes done, and the afternoon spent attending to his normal duties, he walked through the castle and onto the battlements, wanting one last look before he left. To the west, dark clouds were gathering over the mountains, a sure sign that rain would be upon them by nightfall. Villian looked towards the port; his ship standing proud amongst the fleet; ready for action. The dragonhead was visible; waiting to burn its victims. He could picture himself on the ship ordering the flames to destroy their enemies. Better still, he would be on the back of a real dragon at the head of a fleet of dragons.

He made his way to his hiding place and changed into his new clothes; everything secured and hidden as required. He wrapped up his princely clothes and stashed them behind the loose bricks in the wall, wondering when he would wear them again. He took a deep breath as he took a step into the forest, the day's goodbyes in his heart, and an unknown future in his mind.

Unfortunately, he didn't pay as much attention as he should, his head full of future dreams, and great deeds and quests. He didn't notice he was being followed. Arriving at Raykan's hut, he knew instantly something was wrong. The fire was out.

Chapter Twenty-One – Leaving Suntra

Pathanclaw's heart lay heavy as he left Silvarna. They both knew the danger only too well. Thousands of years together were not enough, and the parting was hard. If she'd asked him to stay, he knew, in that moment he wouldn't have been strong enough to refuse. But, his wife, as so often, was stronger than he.

On top of the highest mountain all the dragons had been summoned to witness the gathering. The elders formed a circle. The night of the Festival of Time when the portals opened had arrived. Pathanclaw hoped he was making the right decision. At least if he perished, he knew his wife would keep the family safe, and they would thrive as much as they could under her leadership, and then, in turn his grandson – if he made it back. His hope was that maybe one day a female would be borne, and the history of the dragons would continue.

Long into the night he and Silvarna had talked again about Pathandon. Should he take his grandson with him or leave him here to reign after him if the worst should happen?

Pathanclaw had sighed heavily at Silvarna's response, *"You're right, as usual, my queen."*

The sky had been changing colour all day, the younglings marvelling at this strange change to Suntra's sky. Only the elders had seen the changing colours in their long past, and the excitement had been building, so much so he'd had to roar several times to settle the younglings.

Midnight was approaching and the portal was nearly complete, the swirling colours intermingling to form the doorway he'd entered so long ago. The dragons formed a circle, their wings touching to surround, the King and his General, with Pathandon to the side. They began the complicated enchantment to link the worlds. The colours slowly settled into a funnel of colour which swirled towards the group, encompassing the three dragons; their fates now sealed, unable to turn back.

Pathanclaw could feel the energy of the portal. The magic of old wakening, the power making him feel young again. He concentrated, threading the words and incantations through his mind, twisting and entwining them like the intricate necklaces made by the great jewellers of Arcus.

It was time. The colours stopped swirling to create a solid tower of light. The light flashed and with the final words, they disappeared.

Silvarna stared into the empty space where her family had been. Immediately the dragons knew something had gone wrong.

Chapter Twenty-Two – Escape

Thanan couldn't sleep. Today was the day; the Festival of Time would begin and there would be no going back. His heart was racing with excitement and fear of the day ahead, mixed with sadness and exhilaration from the day's adventures.

The sadness in his heart came from saying goodbye to his mentor, tutor and most importantly his friend. He had to leave a friend to save a friend. A lump formed in his throat and he couldn't stop the tears. He hid his head so no-one could see.

For the final time that morning Thanan had levitated to his position and Tobias had swung his giant body over and their minds had connected. Thanan felt the emotion from his friend, he couldn't work out where his mind started, and Tobias's ended. They were one.

"*What will happen to you once I've gone*?" Thanan asked, fearful of the answer.

"Oh, you don't need to worry about that. They will ask questions, but what happens between us is private and they know this. Besides, who on this planet has the ability to make me answer anything I don't want to?"

Thanan laughed. Tobias was the most important and oldest worm on their world. All the Masters were fearful of him and rarely tried to communicate with him. Thanan had never asked what power his friend had, other than the ability to communicate and pass on his knowledge of the worlds. He was sure that Tobias had only taught him a fraction of what he knew. Even though time was strange in here, it passed the same, but he thought you could probably stay in here until the end of time and never age. Maybe that was why some of the Masters spent so long in here.

Star had once joked how funny it would be if he stayed in the cave for fifty years, and when he came out, he would look the same, but she would look like an old lady. Until she'd realised what she'd said and went quiet. Other than the Masters, no-one ever grew older on Luminosa.

With the laughter gone and a voice full of emotion, Thanan replied, *"Yes, they will soon learn that you never answer questions and will give up, as frustrated as I have been all these years!"*

He could feel the laughter through the wall of sadness.

"Will I ever see you again, Tobias?"

The great worm was silent for a few moments.

"Who knows what this strange universe of ours has planned, young Thanan. I've known many strange events happen across time and worlds."

"I thought you knew everything, Tobias. Are you telling me that you're not the all-seeing, all-knowing worm? That there is actually something you don't know?"

Thanan felt the laughter again, and joined in. It eased the seriousness and sadness of their last meeting.

It was time to go. There was no more to be said, and no more he could learn. They couldn't stay in the cave forever. His friends needed him, and Tobias knew this boy needed to leave. The world was changing again, and his friend would be a bigger part than he could ever know.

"Goodbye, Thanan. I have enjoyed our time together. I hope the Universe conspires so that we meet again. Never let anything come between your friendships, no matter the incentive. You have a long road ahead, and likely harder partings than this one."

Thanan couldn't speak. He didn't have the words yet, he was just a boy. A boy about to take his friends and travel to a place in the hope of finding peace and freedom. Knowing now they would somehow have to return to save the dragons as well as the children.

Tobias had been quiet when he'd asked about the 'Suckers'. He said all would become clear and they didn't have time to discuss the dragons now. Thanan trusted his mentor. If only they had known sooner, maybe they could have done something. But thinking about it later Thanan wondered if this was why Tobias hadn't told them until it was too late for them to turn back. As his mentor reminded him constantly, sometimes not having all the answers made you choose a different path.

The tears fell unbidden onto his pillow. Remembering the heartache of the parting made his whole body ache. The thought of the dragons enslaved when they should be flying high as in Pol's picture. A slight touch on his leg made him look down to see Pol sitting in his hammock, Pol's slight body, barely adding any weight.

He rubbed at his eyes. He didn't want to show his fears and worries to his friend. But, then again, who else if not one of the most important people in his life.

Pol laid their hand on his leg and they stayed in silence for a few more minutes, and gradually Thanan started to feel better, as he always did in Pol's presence.

"Come?" Pol had quietly entered his mind.

A few minutes later, the three friends met up for the last time in the woods, sure in the knowledge that they hadn't been seen leaving. There was no-one to watch over them, so where would they go? As far as the Masters knew they had no magic, and they now knew that past the guards and dragons lay a desert they could never pass. No wonder they didn't have any guards to stop the children.

They went deep into the forest in the direction of the caves where Thanan spent most of his time. The sky was black other than the soft glow from the lantern trees. As they made their way through the dense flower carpet, little bugs lit a path through the flowers. Thanan could see a smile on Pol's face. They were never happier than when they were communicating with nature.

Star stopped in her tracks, and Thanan bumped into her. Dragon hissed at him, and he coughed again as the heat of flame passed his face.

"Oi. Watch where you're going, Star."

The angry retort didn't come and Thanan looked around her.

Pol was standing next to a waterfall with a smile on their face. Thanan looked up but couldn't see the top and it made him feel dizzy. He knew they must have been heading to a waterfall, as the sound had gradually increased as they made their way along the flowery path. The rock face to the side was covered in paintings... paintings of dragons!

His mouth hung open, a bit like the first time he'd arrived in the caves.

"What?" was all Star could manage.

Pol placed their hands on the clawed feet of the red dragon and shimmered. Star and Thanan could feel powerful magic at work. Thanan started to speak to tell Pol to be careful, maybe the Masters would be able to detect the magic. They didn't want to be found out this close to leaving.

But his words were lost on his lips, as the stone wings of the dragon opened to reveal an entrance through the rock.

"Cool," Star exclaimed next to him and started walking forward. Dragon flew ahead as she always did, protecting Star, although she was scary enough on her own.

They walked through the wings of a stone dragon and the immense wings closed behind them. Both mouths dropped in awe. They didn't know that something so beautiful existed.

Water cascaded down the sheer cliffs and collected in the turquoise pool below. Flowers of every colour danced in the gentle breeze. By this point Pol and Star were running through the glades, Pol conducting the flowers into songs. It was daylight in here. A strange light, unlike the colours of their world.

A flock of birds appeared from one of the large lantern trees. Birds. Thanan had heard about birds, but never seen them before, other than the magical ones the children made. Tobias had told him about them in his lessons. He couldn't have imagined they would be so small and beautiful, and so many of them. Dragon was having a great time flying with them. As the birds neared them, Pol raised their hands and they began to sing. Dragon tried to join in, and his attempt at a roar showed his potential. It was impressive.

They spent a few hours enjoying the oasis before Pol signalled it was time to leave. As the dragon wings closed behind them, they knew that it could be a while before they enjoyed such a peaceful time. Pol linked arms with them, the smallest, but clearly the strongest amongst them.

It was time to leave.

Chapter Twenty-Three – Time to go

It was time. The Masters had gathered in the clearing. All the children were unusually quiet, and the ones with creatures subdued. They knew they were witnessing something special. It was a surprise that the Masters had let them attend at all.

The friends were relying on a lot of things to make this plan work. They knew if anything went wrong, they would probably all die, or be parted; either way it amounted to the same thing. The plan for hiding in the caves was a slim one. Maybe they could rescue the dragons if nothing else? Maybe they could help them escape this world or free it from the Masters? There were too many maybes for Thanan's liking.

Thanan looked down as he felt a small hand curl around his. Pol smiled up at him, a strength in Pol's eyes giving him confidence in their plans. Star took his other hand. Dragon was perched on Star's shoulder and she leaned her head in to brush Thanan's face. He felt the roughness of her scales starting to form through the feathers. It was the first time that Dragon had shown him affection. He hoped that Dragon would grow quickly; they would need her protection if this part of their plan worked.

The Masters heads were bowed, all whispering the secrets of magic, the words that would open the portal. The rumour was that they had tried this before and it had never worked. Thanan didn't know who had first said this or how they could have known. The Masters rarely spoke to them. Maybe one of the other worms had told one of their pupils. Perhaps they weren't all as mysterious and frustrating as Tobias. The great worm had been confident it would work this year though – this was the first statement Thanan had ever known him to say with certainty. And this time it was different, the air was alive with magic. The three friends moved closer, as one, making their way forward so they were ready, ready to jump into an unknown world to escape the bonds of this one.

The sky above was no longer settled to one colour. The swirling clouds mingled to form an ever changing kaleidoscope in the sky. The children didn't know where to look, at the sky or the black circle forming before the Masters.

One of the Masters stepped forward with a talisman held high. The Masters were never without them. It moved to the centre of the circle, turning and expanding and as it unfolded, it created a hole into another time or another world, or both. The children gasped knowing they were witnessing great magic, willing to accept the punishment, unable to hold their silence.

Thanan nodded at Pol, and they closed their eyes. Thanan could see Pol's mouth forming the language of magic. He looked at Star and mouthed, 'It's time.' She gripped their hands tighter, whispering to Dragon to be ready and nodding to another child next to her. Star's distraction plan was ready. Thanan squeezed her hand to let her know she was as strong as she looked. Smiling, she released her grip just a little bit.

Star's job was to guide them to the circle and get them through as they concentrated, as well as orchestrating the diversion. This was it.

While they had been getting ready, Triana had been watching them, as she often did. She knew they were up to something. She had been edging closer to the three stupid friends, wanting to know what they were doing so she could tell the Masters and earn their favour. The wrath of the Masters, especially tonight, was not something she wanted to face, even though they were lenient with her, so she had to be sure of what they were doing. Thanan and Pol had closed their eyes now. That horrible blue-haired Star was in the middle with her stupid Dragon. Triana was a little afraid of Star if she was honest. The sheer size of her was unnatural, she was more boy than girl like that weirdo he/she thing that was Pol – who was equally terrifying.

Triana smiled, the three weirdos. That's what she would call them after tonight. She would get the others to chant it every time they passed. Triana smirked as she stood behind them. Maybe if she pushed them into the Masters' circle of magic it would seal their fate.

A flash of light blinded her and as one, everyone shielded their eyes. Everyone except the three, who were ready for it.

The light was their signal. The time was now. Pol raised their arms and as one all three friends lifted from the ground and flew towards the light before the Masters could respond. There was a thunder-crack so loud it sounded like the very planet had split in two. The plan had worked. Then, they were gone.

Chapter Twenty-Four – The Quest Begins

Villian drew his sword quietly and entered Raykan's hut. Smoky air filled his lungs, he realised the fire had recently been extinguished. His waited in the doorway while his eyes adjusted. It didn't take long for him to sweep his gaze across the empty space.

Damn. He didn't have time for this. The hour was fast approaching when he was supposed to leave. Villian's unease grew. It could be no coincidence that this had happened to him tonight; someone had discovered their plans.

A branch snapped behind him and Villian swung round with his sword, ready to deliver the killer blow. The Keeper of Books had his hands in the air, his face belying the shock of having a blade inches from his face.

"What are you doing here?" Villian hissed. He didn't want to alert anyone to their presence. Could the Keeper of Books be the one that had betrayed him? Had he been watching him all along, waiting for the opportunity to stop their plans? Although it wouldn't have been hard, Villian was one of the few users of the castle library.

"Trying to save your life."

If the situation weren't so urgent, Villian would have been shocked at the first full sentence he'd heard the Keeper speak. He had a surprisingly young voice for one so gnarly and old.

"Why do you think my life needs saving?"

"We do not have time for this. Follow me, young Prince. I will lead you to Raykan." At this, he swung his cloak around his body, and stalked past Raykan's hut, heading deeper into the woods. He was holding a strange phial of light above him.

There was no flame that Villian could see.

Could Villian trust him? What else could he do, he reasoned with himself? Surely the Keeper wouldn't have wasted all those years teaching him, only to betray him? Raykan hadn't confided in him the whole plans for the evening, only told him the time to be here and all would be ready. A mistake, Villian could see that now. He should have demanded to know. He was the one setting forth on a quest after all, the one risking his life. Angry with himself, he followed the Keeper of Books, his sword raised, ready to defend them.

As they moved deeper into the woods, he could feel the air changing and felt the odd drip of rain sneak through the thick canopy above. The rain became heavier, masking sounds around him. He'd played and trained in these woods all his life, but tonight they felt sinister and unfamiliar, hidden shadows everywhere. He tried to calm himself, he was a warrior, a Prince. They did not cower like common people; they were brave and courageous. He swallowed his fear and moved deeper into the forest. He kept his sword gripped but loose as he'd been taught, ready to do battle with his foes.

His sword was up before he registered the threat, his training taking over. The clash of swords was unnaturally loud against the night. Villian parried the onslaught of his enemies' weapon, using all his knowledge and strength to gain the upper hand.

He could hear other swords clashing in the night and looking to his left, could see the Keeper battling hard against another hooded man. Villian had a fleeting moment to be impressed by his skills and felt too late the movement behind him. He knew he couldn't get his sword up in time, the masked man in front unrelenting. Villian braced himself knowing that his adventure was over before it began.

The sound nearly deafened him. Metal on metal. He shook his head trying to clear the ringing in his ears.

"Need some help, my Prince?"

"Ironhand!"

"At your service, my Prince."

Villian couldn't waste more time, the blows coming fast and furious. His opponent had skills, that was clear. But Villian was now a man, and now he had Ironhand and the Keeper by his side. He kept his movement random so his enemy couldn't second-guess his path. He stepped to the left ready to end this battle. He sensed his opponent realise his plan, but too late. Their next blow embedded into the tree as Villian intended. That split second was all he needed, and he dealt the killer blow.

The man grunted and went down heavily onto the forest floor. Villian looked around waiting for the next attack, but none came. Other bodies lay on the now damp floor. He looked on in disbelief as The Keeper and Ironhand embraced like old friends, the Keeper's feet lifting off the ground.

Villian didn't have time to ask anything. They needed to find Raykan, but first he wanted to see the face of his enemy.

"Keeper, the light."

A yellow glow emanated from a phial in the Keeper's hand. The Keeper held it above the body on the ground, and Villian peered at his opponent, whilst wondering again how this light didn't have a flame.

"Baynard!" Villian exclaimed, unable to keep the shock from his voice as he turned over the body. It was his father's aide!

Shocked, he stumbled back, what did this mean? Had his father found out and sent his guards to kill his only son? Surely not. Then why? Was he working for someone else? Villian considered Baynard as one of his father's most trusted advisers. He couldn't make sense of it. He'd never liked Baynard, who was constantly snooping into business that didn't concern him and trying to cause him trouble. But to come and attack him! If Villian had known his opponent, he would have been more afraid.

The Keeper touched his arm, "Come on, my Prince, it's more dangerous than I thought. We must get you away. Now."

Villian ran after him, listening and feeling for more enemies. Ironhand took up the rear. Did his father want him dead? Did he actually believe his plans that they had ridiculed? Or was Baynard working for someone else? If so, why would he stop him? Too many questions repeated in his mind and there was not enough time to process them. A few moments later they arrived at a solid wall. For all his years in these woods, Villian did not recognise this place.

"We need to crawl, my Prince."

After scanning the forest for any dangers Villian secured his sword. He crouched down and followed the Keeper, with Ironhand taking up the rear once again. It was a short crawl before they entered what he felt to be a large cave. He couldn't see, the only light was from the Keeper's strange phial of light and this didn't reach to the edges of the cave.

"What is this place?"

"Never mind that, we have no time. Follow me."

He went to protest, but was all too aware they were running out of time. Midnight must nearly be upon them. The Keeper thrust a small leather bound book and one of the phials into his hands and told him to secure it in his backpack as they moved towards a brighter light and into a larger space.

"Raykan, you're safe," Villian was relieved to see his friend standing in the middle of a flat circle of stone as they turned the corner. The Keeper of Books now stood next to him, the large moon illuminating them through a hole in the roof of the cave. Strange light danced around Raykan, as Villian went to speak to him, Raykan threw up a talisman. It settled in the air and started to spin under the words he could now hear his friend and the Keeper muttering to the light. The air was alive with Magic.

Ironhand turned from the sight. Villian followed his gaze to a noise from the way they had come. Ironhand placed a massive hand on his shoulder, squeezed, then turned away and headed towards the unwelcome visitors.

Villian moved forward, his whole body wanting to help Ironhand. But this was all for nothing if he didn't finish what they'd started. Raykan had told him what would happen. Even after all they had said and all he had done, he wasn't truly sure that this would really come to fruition. He wanted to believe in Magic, and that dragons did exist and that he, Prince Villian, would be the one to save his world. He felt the weight of responsibility and stepped forward a man. No longer a young Prince, he would return a King, a Man to save his people.

Noises from the cave alerted him that the enemy were coming. He could hear the clash of swords. He didn't fancy their chances against Ironhand. He had no time to lose. His friends knew the dangers better than he did. He closed his eyes against the rays of light emanating from the circle. He felt his body rising into the air, and the last words he heard were from Raykan, "Good luck, my son."

Villian knew no more.

Part Two

Day One – Pathanclaw

Pathanclaw knew something had gone wrong. In his mind he could only feel one other dragon. Either he'd lost his best friend and General or his grandson. He didn't want to open his mind to find out who he'd lost, but the one remaining might need him. As King, it was up to him to deal with tough situations as much as his old age told him he'd had enough.

He tried to open his mind once again. But he could only hear anguish and pain. This couldn't be how their quest started. Not with death.

Pathanclaw stretched out his wings and checked he'd come through without harm before taking to the air. The light was changing, and they only had hours until it would be night. He looked at the landscape as he flew to find out if it was his friend or grandson who would not carry on this fight. Was this Arcus of the past, at the very dawn of time before humans and dragons existed? They had come here on their escape to Suntra all those thousands of years ago. The mountains were higher than the ones on Arcus when he'd lived there. The volcanos had not yet changed this landscape. The rivers were larger and fuller and a forest covered as far as the human eye could see. He spotted his kin and as he swooped down, it was clear what had happened. A hole scarred the side of the mountain; the General, his friend, had smashed into the unforgiving rock as he arrived onto this world.

The king shook his great head, sadness filling his eyes and heart. For a great dragon, a general, to end this way; they needed him for the war to come and their family, and his heart was weakened for his passing. His heart ached for Bluewing and his mother and all his kin. They would feel it even through the passage of time.

Landing next to Battlewing and Pathandon he could see that his friend's neck was broken. In the throes of the magic he hadn't had chance to slow his pace or to protect himself.

He quickly looked over his grandson; he'd injured his wing. Fear and sadness mirrored in his face.

'How are you, grandson?'

'Well, it's just my wing. Just sprained. I'm sorry. Sorry about your friend, Grandfather. He died saving me. He moved me out of the way and didn't have time to stop or protect himself in time.'

His grandson bowed his head, a weight upon him which would never leave. One day this youngling would rule in his stead. For now, though, he was the grandson who needed his grandfather.

Pathanclaw moved to his grandson and raised his great wing around him. How small he was, it felt like the wrong choice to bring him now. He wished he'd had the strength to leave him behind.

'General Battlewing died in his duty to our family, Pathandon. It could be no higher honour for him and his family name. It is right we feel sadness; we have lost something dear to us. But we must not waste his sacrifice and remember why we are here. He would want us to carry on and succeed in our plans. That is what we must do now, in his honour.'

Pathandon answered bitterly, *'Is it right that one of our kind dies for one of those humans, Grandfather? How is that fair?'*

It was a question Pathanclaw had asked himself repeatedly. He wasn't sure he had an answer when his friend lay dead at his feet. How could a duty to the humans, some of whom his kind had never met, take precedence over them. Responsibility. Promise. Honour. These were the three words that always came to him when he doubted this quest, and the fear of his kin dying out without the females to continue their existence.

'I know it seems wrong, Pathandon, but we have a responsibly to ones who are weaker and more vulnerable than us. Why were we given these great wings, this great knowledge, this compassion for others, the ability to form deep friendships if not to help others? It's our duty to help others, no matter the cost.'

His grandson grew up in that moment. Pathandon nodded his small head which showed the promise of greatness. He did understand, and Pathanclaw felt pride. He wished Pathandon's parents could have lived to feel his pride.

'We must look after our friend now, Pathandon. He deserves a full death honour, but we must do our best. I saw no threat as I flew here. We have time. I would like you to take Battlewing's magic.'

Pathandon looked shocked, *'But that is his family's honour, King Pathanclaw.'*

'It is time for you to be the dragon you will become, Pathandon. It is only right that it is you that takes it. If Bluewing were here, then it would of course pass to him, but we are all kin. I have made my decision.'

They gathered around Battlewing. Pathanclaw looked at his friend, the body broken beneath him, but it still bore his strength and nobility. He nodded at his grandson and Pathandon moved his wing and settled it on Battlewing's once powerful wing. Closing his eyes Pathanclaw spoke the words, the words he had hoped he wouldn't have to say for a millennium.

Pathandon watched as the colour started to drain, first from the tip of the General's tail. That striking blue faded to brown as his grandson secured Battlewing's magic. Even when a dragon died, his magic remained. He knew humans had once experimented and tried to steal this great magic, but no dragon would give up the secret words. They would die first; and many had.

Pathandon stepped back a little unsteadily, the taking of the magic was a strange experience. It took a while for the body to spread the magic, to settle in its new home. Pathandon would need to sleep for a few days. Not ideal, but they needed the time; even though he knew it was the one thing they lacked.

Moving back from the empty shell of his friend, it made it easier to do the next part. The glory of a dragon was not only its sheer size but its colours. Without it he could trick himself into believing it wasn't them any longer.

'Are you ready?' he asked Pathandon.

His grandson nodded. He tried to fly but his wing needed longer to heal. The new magic would help with that. Pathanclaw indicated for him to move far back. When he had, Pathanclaw rose into the air and after one last look at his friend, opened his mouth and let his great fire consume his friend and General as was their way when the Guardian's cave was out of reach. The now dark night sky lit up with dragon fire, the very ground burning beneath the body. Only the gems would remain as a reminder of this great dragon.

Day One – The Group

Thanan couldn't move. He could feel the ground shaking beneath him. It was as if a great weight was holding his body to the earth. His mind quickly caught up with what had just happened. Was he dead? Was this the weight of the ground they had been buried under? Opening one eye, he could see only blue. Nothing else. No trees, no mountain and no sky. They hadn't made it. Despair set in.

Thankfully, the weight on him shifted and the blue colour moved to reveal an eye.

"Holy Dragon. What the dragon fire is it?" Thanan tried to move away from the thing, kicking and flailing his arms about. His brain registered that he could move, so maybe he wasn't dead.

"Oi," came Star's voice.

"Star. Is that you lying on me? Get, off," Thanan shouted.

"Dragon's nuts, you just shouted in my ear." Star rolled off him and finally he could breathe again.

"Holy Dragons, you're heavy."

"Rude. I'm big boned that's all," came Star's angry retort.

Thanan chuckled and then coughed as he tried to get the air back into his lungs. He'd surpassed Star's height slightly a few years ago. But she was still the stronger out of the two, and definitely had the biggest attitude, as well as the higher body mass it seemed.

Now Star had removed herself, he looked up into the sky. The shaking ground had stopped; maybe he'd imagined it. A blue sky like in their old home, but the colour had changed from the dark sky on Luminosa they had just left.

He tuned in to Star's voice, "Is that sky blue?"

"No, it's yellow with a hint of purple! Of course, it's blue."

"Just like Luminosa then? Do you think we really left? Do you think it will change colour later? Do you think we are in the same time?"

"Maybe. I don't know, Star. I hope we have left that place and how many questions can you ask in one go?"

This earned him a nudge in his ribs.

"Didn't Tobias tell you about the world we would go to?" Star said, as she finally sat up and looked at their surroundings for the first time.

"Sort of. Well, not really. Actually, no."

Star turned to look at him. Thanan knew what was coming.

"So, you're telling ME, that WE, jumped through that hole in the world, and YOU didn't know where WE were going?"

"Erm, pretty much."

He only just managed to roll out of the way in time when Dragon swooped and a streak of black appeared on the ground. As he did so, his sleeve was ripped and exposed his arm.

"What the dragons fire is that?" Star said, staring at his arm.

Thanan touched it. It looked like one of the amulets the Masters had worn about their necks, but it had been stretched and wound around his arm. The colours of Luminosa's skies. Each band, a tattooed bracelet on his wrist, inter-woven like rope, the colours so vivid they didn't look real.

"Can you get it off?" Star said, reaching out to touch it.

Thanan rubbed at the tattoo but it was as much a part of him as his skin was.

"Wow, it's looks pretty cool. Like a tattoo some of the children arrive with."

"But what does it mean?" Thanan asked.

"What are you asking me for? Maybe you should have spoken to Tobias a bit more before we made this giant leap into the unknown. It's hardly going to be better than staying on Luminosa if we don't know where we are. And you have some weird tattoo on you – what if the Masters can track us using that?"

Thanan paled thinking about it. "Look it's not my fault, Star. How come I must know everything? If we'd stayed, we would have been split up in two days anyway. Is that what you want? To go back and be parted?"

Thanan was flushed with anger now, masking the creeping fear he was feeling that they had made a big mistake. Tobias had said once they got through, all would become clear. He hoped his mentor was right.

"Look, I'm sorry, Thanan. It's just all such a shock. I wonder if Pol knows what's going on? Wait, where is Pol?" Star said.

They both stood up and looked around, using their hands to shield their eyes from the glare of the sun. They were surrounded by mountains. Neither had ever seen so many, but other children had described them over the years. Places some of them remembered. Thanan couldn't believe the size of them. They seemed to touch the very top of the sky. They were covered in a forest of all different colours and a great river hugged the base.

"What are they?" Star asked pointing at the sky, momentarily forgetting Pol.

"I don't know. They are moving in the same direction as the wind."

Star squinted and scanned the horizon.

"Can you see Pol anywhere?" Star said, not taking her eyes off the sky.

"I cannot see Pol. Do you think they made it through?" Star's voice broke at the end.

Thanan looked at her. Star never got upset. He looked around, but he couldn't see Pol anywhere. "Maybe Pol has arrived on another part of the land? Can you send Dragon out to find them?"

Before she answered, Star sent Dragon into the air and she disappeared into the distance.

"Can you see what she sees yet or speak to her?"

"No, not yet. That should come in time. I've been working hard, but it's too soon yet. I will try and listen to see if Pol is trying to talk to us."

Thanan let Star concentrate. He tried to take in more of their surroundings. They had done it. They were somewhere else. Not in the camp. On another planet, or another time. Or so he hoped. Even though the sky was blue, it was different to theirs. He bent and touched the grass; it was harder, unlike the soft springy moss on their world, but the ground was soft to touch. He hadn't truly believed it would work, despite the confidence Tobias had.

He felt a pang of sadness that he might never see his teacher and mentor, and more importantly his friend again. He wiped away a tear before Star could see. He had to be strong. They needed to find Pol first. They couldn't be hurt, couldn't be dead. Not Pol.

Dragon came back to them and made a noise at Star, "I think Dragon's seen something."

"Which direction?" Thanan said urgently.

"This way," Star said, running towards one of the mountains. As they got closer, they could see Dragon hovering in the sky indicating where they needed to be.

"I think I can see two people," Star said. Even when running hard she wasn't out of breath.

"Two?" Thanan said, slightly breathless and trying not to show it. Fear was gripping his stomach, making it harder to breathe. Why were there two people? Had one of the Masters come through? He tried to form a spell in his mind, not that he could match them, but it felt blocked like in the camp. Surely not. They had no chance if they couldn't perform what little Magic they had.

They came across Pol's small body first. They were very still and lying flat, next to a gently flowing stream that snaked its way from the main river near the mountain. It made them both realise how thirsty they were. Star was the first one to reach Pol. She carefully turned them over, scared at what she would find.

"Pol, are you okay?" Star said, gently shaking their body. Thanan reached them and knelt by Pol. He placed his hand on Pol's head and the tattoo bracelet started glowing. Seconds later, Pol's orange eyes were regarding him. They looked at Thanan and then Star.

In a voice as gentle as the wind Pol pointed at the sky and said, "Clouds."

Star and Thanan's mouths dropped open. Pol could speak.

They didn't have time to say anything further before a groan came from across the stream. Star stayed with the dazed Pol while Thanan ran over.

"Where the dragon fire are, we?"

Thanan couldn't believe what he was seeing. Struggling to sit up was his arch nemesis, Triana.

"Never mind that. What are you doing here, Triana?"

"I don't know what happened. I was standing near you, wondering what you were doing. Next thing there was this flash of light, and I got pushed onto Pol, and then I woke up here. Wherever here is. I'm bleeding, look at my leg."

Thanan looked where she was pointing. It was barely a scratch. She was being an annoying drama queen. He turned his back and stomped back to his friends. He couldn't believe Triana was here. Why her of all people?

"Wait for me. Don't leave me here with that."

He turned his head to see her pointing at Dragon, who was shooting small flames in Triana's direction. Smiling, he turned and carried on.

"Star," Triana shouted, stamping her foot. "Get your Dragon to stop, or else I will turn it to stone."

"If you touch Dragon, Triana, I will snap your scrawny body in half and feed you to my Dragon."

Star was bright red with her hands on her hips. Not a good sign.

"Let's all calm down and work out where we are, Star," Thanan said with a warning in his voice.

"Okay, but if she so much as looks at Dragon the wrong way, I swear I will roast her alive."

"Triana," Thanan said hardening his voice.

"Alright, I wouldn't really do anything. Just stop it breathing fire at me. I'm injured!" Triana said sulkily.

Dragon settled back on Star looking as happy as a Dragon can. Star reached up and stroked her face. Thanan could see even more scales shining under the fading light of the day. She was growing fast.

Pol was looking in wonder at the river and the mountains.

"That's a big mountain," Pol said to no-one in particular.

Triana looked at Star and then Thanan. "It can speak?"

"She's not an IT, Triana. Their name is Pol."

"How am I supposed to know what she is? She does that weird colour change with her eyes and the next minute she's a boy, and then she's back to being a girl again. I mean come on, half the time it's hard to tell what it is. That is weird. And why do you call her them and they? I've always thought it sounded stupid."

Star made a move towards Triana, and she stepped back.

"Look," Thanan said, wishing he could just let Star remove Triana permanently. "We have more important things to talk about," he said, whilst thinking that, Pol talking was the most important thing that had ever happened, bar them coming through a magical portal and still managing to be alive.

"I agree," said Triana, clearly knowing when to back down. Star looked furious and ready to attack.

"Am I at least allowed to ask where we are and what's happened?" Triana asked, as she sat on the ground and tended to her barely injured leg.

Star looked at Thanan. They knew they had to be careful what they told her.

"We've escaped Luminosa, and those evil Masters. Star is turning thirteen in a few days and we needed to get out of there."

"Ah, you didn't want to be parted. How sweet." Triana seemed to suddenly remember where she was. She had no protection from the Masters here. "Sorry. Star. I'm sure I would have thought about doing the same when I got to your age."

"You're what, ten?"

"Ten and a half," Triana said, straightening her back.

"Well, whatever age you are, it wouldn't be long before you had to leave that evil place. If you actually had any real friends, you might care that you're being forced to leave them!"

Thanan touched Star's arm. He needed to calm the situation down and distract everyone. They had to make a plan. What kind of a plan he would figure out as he went along.

"First, we need to find some food. I don't know about any of you, but I'm starving. Can you see any food bushes?" Thanan asked.

"We have food. Pol, have you got the food?" Star asked.

Pol appeared to have lost their voice again as they looked around and shook their head.

"Oh, erm, I think I might have knocked a bag off her when I was pushed into her," Triana said, taking a step back.

"Right, that's it," Star said and started chasing after Triana. Dragon was swooping down as Triana screamed.

This was a great way to let everyone know they were here, wherever here was. "Star, Triana, Dragon, back here NOW and shut up, all of you." Thanan hissed in anger, his temper finally breaking.

Recognising his imminent explosion, they all returned, Triana a few paces behind a sheepish looking Star. "Sorry Thanan, but that was all the food we had, and I'm starving."

"There must be food around here somewhere. Send Dragon out to look for any signs of food and other people – we need to make sure we are safe here. We don't know how long it will be before it goes dark and we need to find some shelter. Meanwhile, we can look around and see what we can find. Pol, take the skeins and fill them with water."

With that, everyone got on with their tasks, even Triana who had the decency to look sorry about the food, although he suspected it was only because she was going without.

There were plenty of bushes and trees around, not the kind that were on Luminosa though. After searching nearby without leaving the sightline of the small group they hadn't found any food bushes anywhere. Dragon had come back with nothing. They'd decided to let Dragon rest before sending her back out later. Strangely, even though Dragon was magical, Star and she were linked in so many ways. If Dragon was tired, so was Star, but they could somehow shift the balance of energy between them. There was so much they didn't understand and now they had left how would they find out what was possible?

"What's this on the tree? Could that be food?" Star said.

They all looked up into the tree, something yellow was hanging from a branch.

"Do you think that's food?"

They stood underneath the tree, staring at the yellow things hanging down. Star's stomach rumbled and Triana sniggered until Star glared at her.

Star looked at Dragon. "Can you knock them down?"

Dragon leapt into the air and reaching the yellow things she gripped one with her talon and it squashed and fell from the tree landing on Triana's head.

Star was the first one to start laughing and the others soon joined in, eventually even Triana saw the funny side. It had been a long evening and their adventures had only just begun.

Day One – Villian

Something was digging in his back. Villian moved carefully, worried that he'd broken his body. That wouldn't be a good start to his quest. He sat up, his eyes adjusting to the light of the day. It had been night when he'd left. His heart felt heavy when he thought about his home and his friends. He remembered now that he'd heard other people arriving in the cave. Would Raykan, The Keeper and Ironhand be able to defend themselves? On second thoughts he should be worrying about the enemy; Ironhand was a scary warrior.

The ground shook underneath him. A quake? A landslide from one of the mountains? What was it? Moments later it settled. He waited a few minutes, but the ground had stopped shaking.

Villian looked around him. He was next to a lake, surrounded by forest, and he could hear birds in the nearby trees. Had he truly left his world as Raykan had told him he would? Or had he just moved in time? This world was remarkably familiar. Time was exactly what he needed to work out his next move. He was thirsty; the fight before entering the portal had left his throat dry and his body aching. He took off his backpack and sword and placed them close whilst he knelt into the river. After sniffing it, he cupped the fresh water and drank until his thirst was quenched. His eye caught a flash of colour on his wrist.

"What?" He said out loud before he could stop himself. He looked around, afraid to attract unwanted attention until he'd surveyed his new surroundings. A bird sounded in the tree, the only reaction to his voice. It appeared he was alone.

He wondered when he would stop feeling surprised. Raykan had told him that he would need the tattoo bracelet to return, he just hadn't really thought it would look like this. Magic. Again, the word made him tingle with excitement. The colours of the tattoo glinted in the sun as he moved his arm trying to see how it had formed on his arm. It was like a woven bracelet had been melted onto his skin. He tentatively rubbed his fingers over the top of the tattoo, marvelling at the colours and detail. It looked like a metal bracelet rather than just a tattoo – but his arm was smooth to the touch. His father had the best silversmiths in the land and they would be envious. As he turned his arm it looked like the dragon blood clasps on the book fixed the bracelet in place. Ironhand would pay him a fortune just for one look.

He realised this was the swirling mass of colour that had created the magic portal. He would use this to return to his world and save Arcus, if only he knew how to use it. Everything Raykan had said had come true so far, so he had no reason to doubt that he would find what he sought in this world.

So, all he needed to do was find someone who knew how to open the portal, find the dragons and persuade them to come back whilst making sure they didn't all die when they returned. Raykan had said all would be revealed when he arrived, but when Villian saw the look of worry in his old friend's eyes, he'd chosen to ignore it. The alternative of doing nothing was not an option. Once he'd achieved all these tasks, he needed to return to his world and save everyone. He was starting to realise exactly what he'd taken on. Ideas of grandeur, youth and saving the world were all very good when you had a castle and thousands of soldiers.

Thirst quenched, food was his next thought. He'd already established he needed to regroup and come up with a plan. That would take time. His training by all his teachers had involved patience, not to rush into situations without using his brain and thinking of all the options. As keen as he was to get on, he knew his body needed to recover from the fight, and he needed to analyse the events of the last few hours. Meeting his future wife, The Keeper's role in the plans, Baynard's betrayal – was his father involved? Ironhand's involvement? Villian cleared his mind. Later, first to secure his surroundings and find food to sustain him on his quest.

He spent the next few hours setting up a camp on the outskirts of a small forest and setting traps. He'd seen rabbits scurrying in the woods and birds called their warnings. This forest was clearly full of life, as was his home world. He created a small shelter using branches and collected rocks to create a safe area to light a fire. He didn't know what dangers this place held, but if the temperatures dropped in the night, he would need fire. It was a risk, as he didn't want to alert anyone to his presence. But he also needed to meet the person who was going to help him.

Dusk was approaching as he finally relaxed into his temporary home. Opening his backpack, he took out the book and phial the Keeper had thrust into his hands. He laid them on the ground in front of him while he took out some dried meat. He had a good week's worth of provisions, but the traps were set. He only had himself to rely on and once this quest started, he didn't want to waste precious time hunting. Who knew how long he had before the enemy attacked the castle on Arcus?

Chewing on the meat, he stretched out his legs, thankful that he'd laid a fire. The air was starting to turn chilly as it moved towards dusk, and although a light mist of rain had started, his shelter would keep him dry. He first looked at the phial. It fitted comfortably into the palm of his hand, the size of one of the phials Raykan used for his herbs. Made of thick clear glass there was nothing unusual about it other than the light it emitted when he touched it.

Putting it down, the soft glow immediately went out. So, it obviously worked by human touch, maybe the heat from his hand. Villian was a bit disappointed. He would have liked to have said a magic word, although since he didn't know the magic word, it wouldn't have been of much use to him right now. He placed it carefully into one of the secret pockets and looked at the book.

The small book was bound in leather, with a simple piece of frayed twine to secure it. It had no distinguishable marks that Villian could see. No fancy clasps like the other book. Opening it, he counted twenty pages filled with neat tiny writing, a few drawings breaking up the text. The problem was he couldn't read it, the language was not one he was familiar with. Turning a page, he was shocked that one of the pictures was the coloured tattoo bracelet he was wearing – was wearing the right word? He tried to work out any familiar letters, but it was no good. Another mystery.

Villian yawned. He needed to get some sleep; his sight was blurry from tiredness, his body weary to the bone. These would have to wait until the morning. He pulled his blanket over him and the moment his head touched his rucksack he was asleep, his dagger hilt gripped in his palm.

Day One – The Group

They were free. Sort of. They'd managed to eat some of the food from the trees, but it wasn't enough. Night was fast approaching and they were out in the open with no protection when the fine rain started.

"Great," said Triana. "This just keeps getting better. I'm tired, hungry, lost in some stupid place with nowhere to sleep and now it's raining."

"Why don't you magic up some shelter if it's that bad?" Star retorted.

"Don't you think I've been trying to think of something that would help? We don't learn spells to make food or shelter."

"Well, what do you learn then? What's the point of it if you cannot even help yourself? Thanan, can you not do anything?"

"I hate to agree with Triana, but we are not taught things like that. We learn how to create magic but not always what we're doing with it."

"Well, that's stupid. Didn't any of you ever ask? How can you make a spell if you don't know what it's for?"

Triana looked at Thanan, and for once they were thinking the same thought. You never, ever questioned the magic you were taught. You were given a set of instructions on how to form the colours, but most of the time you didn't know what that was creating. The odd time they were told it was only to create silly things like when Triana had changed the taste of his food.

"What about the levitation spell, Thanan, surely you know others?"

Triana looked sharply at him, "How do you know a levitation spell?" Thanan frowned at Star. Great. All they needed was Triana knowing he knew more than he was letting on. Tobias had helped him with some forms unbeknown to the Masters.

"Ha, as if you can levitate. You're just pretending to know more than me?" Triana said.

"Yes, he can. Show her Thanan."

Thanan could see this argument would go on for hours and he didn't have the energy. He had tried earlier and the magic hadn't come, but then they had just arrived, and his head wasn't clear. He closed his eyes and formed the colours until they linked to make the spell and released.

"Come on then, Thanan. Let's see you fly."

Frowning, he tried again. Nothing. Opening his eyes, he looked at Pol, who shrugged. It wasn't them stopping the magic.

"It doesn't work," Thanan said, a little worried.

"As if it ever did."

"You try then, Triana, if you're so much better."

Looking smug, she closed her eyes and minutes later opened them again with a frown.

"It doesn't work! Have we lost our magic on this world? How in dragons' teeth are we going to manage without our magic?"

"Well, it wasn't as if you knew anything useful anyway," Star retorted.

"Pol, do you know anything about it? Can we get it back?" Thanan asked.

Pol just shrugged again.

"Great, ask the mute weirdo what we should do! You're all so stupid. You've sent us to a strange world which we don't know. We have no food, no idea what to do and now no magic."

The others kept quiet for once. It was true. The full realisation was hitting home. Inside though, Thanan was sure there was a plan. Tobias wouldn't have encouraged him, taught him what to do to leave Luminosa if he thought they were just going to die here. They might have well stayed and taken their chances being separated, if they were just going to die here.

"NO," Thanan said it so loud it made them jump. "No," he said again more softly but with steel in his voice. "There is a reason for all of this. We just need to get through the night and then the morning will show us the way." Or so he hoped.

"Well. While you lot have been messing about, I've sent Dragon out. She's seen something, but it's a long walk. I vote we go in that direction. We cannot stay here all night in the cold."

They made a sorry bunch of travellers as they followed Star. Triana stayed at the back planning how she was going to get away from these freaks and pay them back for getting her into this, and wondering who did push her into the Pol. Was it part of the plan?

Day One – The Meeting

Villian awoke instantly, sensing something was wrong. He strained to hear what had woken him. There it was again. Could it be a bird? A creature, large or small in the forest, but to his trained ears it sounded like people.

A noise. Someone or something was out there. Heart pounding, he carefully and quietly slid the blanket off his body and gripped his dagger.

Whispering now; definitely human voices. A girl he thought, and a boy. He was sure he could make out more than two sets of footsteps. Were these the people he was supposed to meet? No matter, he had to defend his camp. Nothing could come in the way of his quest. He had to work out if they were friend or foe, and quickly. The fire was still glowing, and he decided to leave it. They must have seen it. He cursed himself, but he'd had little choice other than to build the fire. The night was cold, and a film of dew had already formed.

He couldn't leave his shelter without showing himself. He shuffled back as far as he could, hoping they wouldn't see him straight away and it would give him the element of surprise. He gripped his dagger.

"This way." The words were shouted, not someone trying to sneak up on him then. Who were these reckless people stumbling in the night? Did they not know the potential dangers?

"Will you be quiet?" Came the angry hushed voice of a male.

A hissed retort came back, no quieter, "I can see a fire and I'm freezing and hungry. Just you stop me."

Their pace quickened and seconds later what sounded like a stampede of horses arrived at his camp. Villian pushed himself further back into the shelter. Moments later the light from the fire was extinguished as a figure stood between him and the fire. How silly. In a flash, Villian moved from crouching, to securing the dagger firmly in place around the person's neck. They were much smaller than him, a child, and he held them easily, the dagger tip pressing down into their neck.

"Hey, what are you doing? Get off me!" came the girl's voice. Villian nearly let go when she attempted a well-aimed kick to his shin.

"Do that again and I will slit your throat." He said this in his most menacing and commanding voice. The girl went still.

Over her head he saw three more figures on the other side of the camp, open mouthed at the sight their companion with a dagger to her throat.

"Who are you? And what are you doing here? Tell me now or I will slit her throat." Again, Villian used his commanding Prince's voice.

"Will you stop saying that?" the girl cried. Villian pressed the dagger deeper and she made no further reply.

Two of her party were as tall as him, although they looked much younger. The girl in the middle was tiny; a mere child. They were all children. What were they doing out here? One had bright blue hair and, weirdly, a grin on her face. The boy's shocked face had turned to one of satisfaction. Why were they reacting like that? He had their companion at his mercy.

Their manner of dress looked odd as well, like the peasants his father wouldn't allow into the castle, but he didn't have time to focus on all of that. He quickly scanned them for weapons. Nothing that he could see.

"Answer me. Now. You've been warned."

Their faces changed a little at this. Moments later, the boy spoke.

"My name is Thanan, this is Star." He pointed to the girl with the long blue hair. "This is Pol," pointing at the child,

“And the person you’re holding captive is Triana. We don’t mind if you cut her throat as none of us like her and she shouldn’t be here, and so far she’s been a pain in the backside of a dragon.”

The one called Star giggled.

Day One – Companions

Villian didn't know what to make of these strange children. Why didn't they care if he killed their companion? What kind of a world was this? He was beginning to worry that Raykan had sent him to the wrong place and the wrong time.

He felt the one he was holding, Triana the one named Thanan had called her, bristling with indignation at the comment. He could feel her whole body tense and he didn't think it was because of his dagger. He was thrown as to what to do. But these were merely children. How much harm could they do? Despite being outnumbered, they had no weapons and clearly no idea that they were in so much danger.

"What are you doing here?"

"Escaping," Thanan said. He appeared to be the leader of this odd bunch.

"Escaping from what?"

The blue haired girl said, "Look we've escaped from a wicked world where these Masters kept us all captive, and if we hadn't left, myself and Thanan would have been goners, as once you reach thirteen you disappear. And so, here we are. If you could just let us sit around your fire and warm up, and then tell us where the food bushes are, we will be on our way in the morning."

Villian tried to take all this in. The girl was speaking extremely fast. She had her arms folded and looked quite menacing. She was as tall as him and only twelve years old if what she said was true. He marvelled at her story. The Masters had to be one and the same, the ones that had ruined, were ruining, his world. These children had been kept captive and escaped. They could be extremely useful to him. Were these the ones who were supposed to lead him to the dragons? So much information to take in.

"What are these food bushes you speak of?" Villian asked.

"What do you mean, what are they? Please tell me you have food bushes here? How are we going to eat? We are starving. That one," the girl, Star pointed at his captive, "knocked the bag out of Pol's hand when we travelled here and we have had nothing to eat all day other than some yellow mush out of a tree, which actually tasted quite nice."

The boy, Thanan, nudged her.

Villian nearly smiled. He was beginning to like this girl; in fact, he was warming to them all.

"I don't know what you mean about food bushes. Certainly, fruits grow, if that's what you mean? But I normally eat from food grown in the ground or meat that is killed, and..."

"You kill animals?" Star interrupted him.

"Yes, what else would you eat?"

Star looked at Thanan.

Villian thought that these children really had no clue. These food bushes sounded interesting though. When the time came for battle, more food was a constant need to keep an army marching. Was this something they'd used Magic to create?

Villian couldn't believe he was standing in a different time, with a dagger to the throat of a girl, while other children's only concern was about food. It was time to take control.

"Look, I get the feeling that you children are not here to cause me harm. I will let your... erm," he was going to say friend, "companion go, if you promise not to do anything silly. I will kill you all without a moment's hesitation if I sense danger. Is that clear?"

All heads nodded, even his captive, who then cried out when the tip of the dagger nipped her neck. Villian sighed and let her go. It was quite clear to him that these children bore him no ill will. In fact, it was becoming obvious that he needed to teach them a few things about the world. His quest had to come first, but these children knew where these Masters were; maybe they could help him find the dragons. The boy, Thanan had mentioned dragons – they knew what they were.

He gestured for the children to sit around the fire. The boy called Pol still hadn't spoken. Villian kept the fire between him and his new companions, in case they decided to attack, although looking at them they were a sorry state, wet, cold and thoroughly miserable. Once more, after wood had been added to the fire, he passed around some of the cured meat for them to eat. His camp was under a canopy, so it afforded enough shelter for them all. He hid a smile as he saw them turn it over and sniff it before looking at each other. Thanan was the first one to try it. The others stared at him and after he nodded, they all started eating.

"This is actually quite nice. What is it?" Star asked.

"Cured Pig."

"What's a pig?" Triana asked before ripping a chunk of meat off and chewing like she'd hadn't eaten in weeks.

"You don't know what a pig is?" Villian was fascinated, what kind of a place had these children come from?

Thanan proceeded to tell them about the food bushes on their world. They had never seen any animals, although they'd heard about some. He kept quiet about the dragons and the birds he'd seen when Pol had taken them to that secret place. On Luminosa the creatures only tended to be dragons or lizards. He realised they had already said too much to this stranger and Triana, but the stranger did seem like someone they could trust. Thanan looked him over: well built, with an air of confidence about him. His clothes were odd, and Thanan felt envious and a little conscious of his own rags.

"Who are you anyway?" Thanan suddenly blurted. He felt himself go a little red at the outburst.

Villian smiled at him though and nodded, acknowledging the question as more sensible than that of pigs. As they had been eating, he'd wondered what to tell this strange group. It appeared they had been honest about their journey so far, and clearly needed looking after, as well as being able to give him information. He decided to go with the truth.

"My name is Prince Villian of Arcus. I'm on a quest to restore peace to my world."

He looked at them all, waiting for someone to speak.

Finally, the boy Thanan spoke, "You're a Prince? How old are you?" He'd heard stories of princes and castles from Tobias.

"A good deal older than any of you. I'm nearly eighteen. Yes, I am a Prince. My father is King of Arcus and I will be his successor and marry Lady Cartina when I return victorious."

Star started giggling first, and one by one they all joined in. Even the one called Pol sniggered quietly behind his hand. Although looking at him again his features had changed somehow – more feminine! What strange witchcraft was it? At first Villian felt angry at their ridicule, but realised that to a stranger's ears it did sound rather fanciful. He soon joined in their laughter, keen to keep them on side, and so tired he certainly didn't care that they were laughing at him. He needed sleep.

"Okay, I think we need to keep the noise down. Who knows what dangers lie out there. We must be careful until we have surveyed the area."

"Oh, don't worry. There isn't another person for many miles, and if I could use my magic I could show you, and Star's stupid creature checked anyway," Triana said.

Star elbowed her hard in the ribs.

"Oi, what did you do that for?" Triana shouted.

"How do you know there is no-one else here? You cannot have travelled that far on foot? What creature?" Villian asked, feeling like maybe he'd misjudged these innocent looking children. He pretended he hadn't heard the quip about magic.

"Triana, you really do have such a big mouth," Thanan said.

"What?" Triana said, through her mouthful of food.

"Look, we're not trying to be untruthful, but we have only just met you. I promise we're good people – well apart from

Triana," Thanan said, as Triana rolled her eyes. He hoped Villian hadn't realised what she was talking about, but he'd seen his eyes widen. "But it is so late, and we've all been through so much today, please can we talk about this in the morning when we've had some sleep?"

Villian considered his request. For a boy, there was a lot to admire about him. He reminded him of himself, old beyond his years. As a prince this was expected of him. He wondered at this Thanan's story and what had happened to make him so wise beyond his years, although his world sounded a hard one for a child to grow up in.

"I accept your request, Thanan. Maybe it would be wise for us all to get some sleep. I too could benefit from some rest. But I still think it would be prudent for us to take it in turns to guard the camp, regardless that you believe there are no dangers lurking."

"I vote Triana takes the first watch," Star said grinning.

"That would seem fair. It looks like she has a good hour of eating left," Villian said, to the mirth of the others.

Triana stood up and stamped over to a nearby tree, taking one of the blankets with her and still grumbling, settled herself against the back of a tree, but still near enough to feel the warmth of the fire.

"Oi, that's mine," Star said, about to get up.

"That's okay. You can borrow one of mine." Villian handed her one of his spares from his backpack.

Thanan looked at Star and raised his eyebrow. Ever since Villian had said he was a prince she had gone all 'girly'. Thanan looked at Pol, who had been quiet as a mouse since they'd arrived in Villian's camp. The discovery that Pol could talk and that none of them could use magic had been a shock to say the least. But now Pol could talk, maybe they could find out more. They hadn't been able to use their minds to communicate since they'd arrived. This planet acted like the Suckers on Luminosa – it made him feel sad and scared.

They all bedded down for the night, grateful for a full belly and warmth, Thanan thinking that the group had said too much and Villian wondering about the creature and more importantly Magic.

Day Two – Danger

Thanan woke to the rumble, his whole body vibrating in time with the earth. He heard Star swear and couldn't help but smile even though he had a growing dread inside him. Quickly he got to his feet, as the others were startled awake, even Triana, who was supposed to be on watch. It was pitch black bar the light from the fire, which didn't seem to penetrate much beyond their small camp.

"What's happening?" Thanan asked, directing his question at Villian.

"Quake in the ground by the feel and sound of it."

"State the obvious why don't you?" came Triana's whiny voice. "Of course it's a quake in the ground. But what's causing it and are we in danger?"

Villian shared the same look with Thanan, a small smile catching the side his mouth. Thanan was warming to him more and more.

"Hold on while one of us looks into our crystal ball. Oh wait, I think I know. The planet is rebelling against you being on it, Triana. This planet clearly has taste," Star said.

Pol let out a short laugh, which shocked their friends more than the danger from the quake. Closing their mouth, Pol looked serious again and bent down to place their hand on the ground. Shutting their eyes, their brow furrowed with concentration. By this time everyone was staring at Pol. They weren't sure if it was a trick of the light, but a glow seemed to be coming from Pol's hand.

"This planet is dying."

No-one spoke as they let the words sink in.

"What are you talking about?" Triana demanded, "How can a planet die? And how would you know that anyway? I know you're a bit of a freak."

"Oi!"

Star strode over and calmly side swiped Triana's legs so she fell back flat on her backside. The noise of Triana's complaining could probably be heard for miles.

"Triana, will you shut up," Thanan whispered through gritted teeth. "We don't know if anyone else is around and you need to shut up, now."

He put his hand up to stop her replying.

"Enough, you're going to get us all killed, and if you don't, so help me, if you don't stop putting us in danger, we will leave you here."

His words finally shut her up, although she glared at the smirking face of Star. Thanan gave Star a look and she showed defiance in her eyes before nodding.

Villian watched this display with interest. His father would be impressed with this boy. There was a tug at his heart, and a flash of anger as he thought of his father and the meaning of his personal bodyguard attacking him. His friends. His wife to be. He had to complete his quest and get back to them as soon as possible.

Before anyone else could speak, the rumbling got worse and a loud crack sounded, as if the planet was splitting in two. They covered their ears. Next, a flash of light in the distance marked the start of a terrifying race to daybreak.

"What in dragon's fire was that?" Star asked. Thanan noted that she moved closer to Villian as she said this.

"A volcano. We have them on Arcus. But they have been dormant for many thousands of years. They say that dragons were created from the fire of the planet." Villian had noted her use of the word dragon – they knew what dragons were – they had mentioned them before and it was not a coincidence,

"What are we going to do?" Triana asked.

"We need to move away from here and fast. It looks a long way away, but I don't know how far the smoke and lava fire will travel. There is no wind now, and the rain has stopped, but if it picks up then we are in great danger."

"What's lava?" Triana asked.

"A river of fire," Pol said. Thanan wondered how they knew this.

"Great," Star exclaimed. "Maybe we need to think about getting out of here?"

"But where are we going to go? It's so dark out there."

Thanan reached into his backpack and took out the phial of light, as Villian reached into his secret pocket for his. Star and Thanan stared at Villian.

"Where did you get that from?" they said in unison. Star's phial had smashed when they'd arrived.

Thanan held up his phial to Villian, they were identical. Shock registered on both their faces.

"Never mind that. We need to move," Villian said. Had these phials come from the same place? If so, did the Keeper know about the other planets? How had he got the phial? So many questions but he couldn't think about them now.

"Do you think it's safe to travel by the light? It's a good way to announce exactly where we are if there is anyone else here," Star said.

"I don't think we have much choice, Star. Judging by the sound of the quakes and the light in the distance, I think we have to move, and fast."

Decision made, they quickly assembled their few possessions. Star filled the skeins with fresh water from the stream, and to the sound and feel of the rumbling ground, they made their way in the opposite direction. They covered ground quickly, but it didn't take long before the smell of smoke reached them. Villian took the lead with Star; Dragon was keeping her distance as they didn't want this new companion to know about Dragon yet. The time wasn't right, they had to be sure of this Villian. Could he be trusted? They might need Dragon to help them escape.

Thanan took up the rear of the group. He felt a presence behind him and kept turning. He felt as if they were being watched.

"This is not looking good. We need to try and get some shelter somewhere until it passes. If we get surrounded by the ash cloud, we don't stand a chance. We need to find a cave," Villian said, as he stopped, and they all gathered together, panting and coughing.

Thanan held the phial up. They had been following the river, but on the other side was now a jagged sheer rock face. There was no way they would be able to climb it. Without magic they couldn't fly over it. He felt frustrated. If only they could use magic, they would be able to get to safety. The air around them was getting thicker, they needed to get out of open ground.

"Star, why don't you send Dragon ahead and see if she can see an opening?" Triana asked.

Thanan was about to shout at Triana, but Star beat him to it, "I know what you're going to say Thanan, but we haven't got time to keep the secret. If we don't get to safety soon, we could all die."

Thanan was reluctant to show their hand, but what choice did they have?

Dragon quickly appeared above Star's shoulder, and Villian jumped back.

"Dragon's fire. You have a dragon?" Villian couldn't keep the shock and awe out of his voice. This was his first ever glimpse of a real dragon, the first confirmation of what he'd dreamed of all his life. It was true. There really were dragons in this world. He didn't realise they would be so small!

"She's not a real dragon!" Triana's voice interrupted his thoughts. "She's Star's creature that's all."

"That's all. Well, she could burn your hair off and bite your head off bit by small bit like a real dragon. Shall I show you?" Star said with a glint of mischief in her eye.

"Star, enough. Just send Dragon ahead. We haven't got time for all this."

Duly chastised, Star spoke to Dragon and she flew off, following the river. They stood in silence, lost in their own thoughts. Thanan glanced at Villian. He was staring in the direction Dragon had gone. Thanan mused it must have been the first time he'd ever seen one, even though he said his quest was to take dragons back to his home world. But he doubted Villian had thought they would be so small. If they were not in so much danger it would have made him chuckle. It would take some explaining later. He was worried they had broken trust with him. Thanan realised he was out of his depth with what to do next. They might need this prince. Danger seemed to be a constant companion since they'd arrived.

"Where is she? Some use she is. Probably flown off and left us to our fate." Triana said.

Star ignored her, which was frightening in itself. She looked worried about Dragon.

A gust of wind brought in choking smoke and they struggled to clear their throats.

Without warning, Pol started running in the direction Dragon had gone.

"Pol, where are you going? Wait."

But Pol didn't wait, they just kept on running. The others had no choice but to follow, grateful at least to get away from the smoke.

Villian couldn't believe how fast Pol was, and he thought he was a good runner. He turned slightly to make sure the others were keeping up. His foot caught on a large stone and he went down heavily, grunting at the impact. The phial flew out of his hand but thankfully didn't smash. Before he knew it Star and Thanan were at either side helping him up, and Villian scooped it up as they passed. They carried on their chase, Triana managing to moan even as she ran.

Finally, Pol stopped, and gasping, they all slowed to a stop. The thickening smoke was affecting them all now and the constant coughing was becoming overwhelming. A strong gust of wind came from nowhere and sent the smoke in another direction and the way ahead was clear.

Thanan grabbed Pol's arm to stop them running again. They turned to look at him and pointed towards the mountain. He held up the phial and strained to see against the smoky air. There was a black hole in the side of the mountain and Dragon was hovering nearby.

"Is that a cave, Pol?"

Pol nodded.

"Right, everyone. Through the river and follow Pol."

"I'm not getting my feet wet," Triana said through her coughing.

"Fine. Stay here then," Star replied and ran off following the others who had already set off to follow Pol.

Triana looked around into the dark night, squinting into the darkness. She was sure she could see a light in the distance. No, not a light. Her eyes widened as she realised it was a pair of eyes! Massive red eyes glaring back at her. A monster! She screamed and ran after the others.

Day Two – Pathanclaw

Pathanclaw flew for hours trying to understand where they were. This world was a mixture of flat endless plains and huge mountains. Some of the blackened plains were a clear indication that this was not a settled world. It was still changing and forming, or as he suspected, ending. He saw plenty of signs of life despite the changing nature of the landscape. Herds of beasts and flocks of birds cried out, desperately trying to get away at the appearance of his mighty wings forming shadows on the land.

He would take food back to his grandson later; he would need his strength to heal. Luckily, dragons healed quickly, and the addition of the new magic would help. In a day he would be ready to fly. The death of his friend Battlewing lay heavy on his heart, but he'd given his life for his grandson and there was no bigger honour for a Blue. The decision of a king was never easy; but this devastating loss so soon made him question why he had decided to take his family and protect the humans. Why didn't he stay with Silvarna and live a long happy life? It was difficult to describe the urge he felt. The pull to help the humans was too strong.

With all the events so far, his mind had been on other things. Now he thought once again about their goal and he realised something had changed. He landed on the side of a rocky mountain, his giant claws securing him. His great head turned in all directions. Something. Unless his old age and senses were defying him, he could detect humans, young humans who had a different smell.

Could these be the ones Raykan had promised to send? He felt a rumble underneath him. The planet had stirred, and he wondered if the magic they had used to transport here had unsettled the delicate balance.

His far-seeing eyes scanned the horizon. The heat inside the mountain was visible to his trained eyes. This did not look good. He had lived in the times of ferocious volcanoes. Not many things posed a danger to dragons – but the planet's fire could cause even their undoing; after all, it was where they were made.

The volcano was going to erupt, he was sure of it. Looking at the direction the lava and fire were likely to go, he decided it did not pose a threat to Pathandon. He would be out of danger where he was. Maybe the smoke would reach him, but that would not be a problem. He decided to circle around, pick up some food and warn his grandson. Then he would track down the humans, who might need his help.

As he flew, he marvelled at the fragility of humans. They were a weak design in many respects but their determination to survive and thrive were what set them apart. They had the ability to change their landscape beyond recognition, to kill ruthlessly and also protect other species with their lives. They possessed great compassion to save and protect. Dragons and humans were very much alike. Although dragons never killed for no reason, other creatures had to die so they could live. This was the natural order of the world. Their species were here to keep order, although he admitted that they were failing to achieve this. He would change their future and he would bring order back. He needed to leave a settled world for his family. Is that not what they should all do for the ones who came after?

Pathanclaw tried not to look at the scorched patch where his friend and commander had met his death. To die so needlessly. It caused him great pain.

Pathandon looked grateful for the food he had brought. After they had eaten, he brought his grandson up to date on what he knew. His responsibility was to train this young dragon to be a leader one day.

"So, there are humans on this planet, young humans?"

"But how can they be here? You've said we are not in the right time on Arcus. Do you think there are many of them? Maybe a whole tribe?"

Pathanclaw smiled to himself. Tribe was one of the old names humans had used for their pack and came from the stories passed to the young dragons.

"I think there are only a few of them. I cannot detect more than four – but as we know our powers do seem to be more limited here."

"We need to protect them, grandfather. If this volcano does vent its anger on the land, we will need to make sure they get to safety."

This pleased Pathanclaw, that his grandson's immediate thought was to protect the humans. It was promising, although, he wouldn't expect less from one of his clan.

"Yes, your wing seems to be healing nicely. Very soon you will be well enough to fly, and your new magic should have settled."

"I think it would be best if you go and find the humans and make sure they are well and when I'm healed we will speak to them together."

Pathanclaw didn't think it would be as simple as that. To his knowledge, humans had not come across dragons in thousands of years. Did they even know about the strong bond that they held all those years ago? The humans would fear them and that could cause them to do stupid things; he had known this in the past. As well as being intelligent, humans had the capacity to be very, very stupid. He hoped his friend had prepared them for this meeting.

Pathandon interrupted his thoughts, *"That's, of course, if you think that sounds like what we should do. You are the head of the family."*

Pathanclaw turned his head to eye his grandson. *"When did you become so wise young dragon? Your parents would be proud. You're right of course. I will go and check on the humans and report back as soon as I can; if that pleases, my lord."*

Pathanclaw bowed his great head in mock reverence and if Pathandon had been a human he would have blushed.

"Fine. Do as I command, and you will go far," Pathandon replied. It was good to hear some humour back in his grandson's voice.

Their bellowed laughter felt good after the emotions of the last day. He couldn't be prouder of this king in the making.

Late in the night the volcano erupted and Pathanclaw sensed it was time to continue his search. He leapt into the air, his great wings disturbing the loose rocks below him. He could feel a sense of panic or urgency in the young humans.

The smoke was getting thicker, which would not be good if the humans were out in this. In the distance he spotted five figures moving fast. Five; he tested his senses. He could still only detect four. He couldn't understand what the fifth one was. It seemed to be with the humans, so it didn't seem to pose a threat. Interesting.

He didn't want to get too close as they would hear him coming, although a dragon could ride the thermal waves in the air and silently swoop on their prey. The humans were already running in terror from the volcano. The lava would not reach this far but the smoke was thickening moment by moment. They needed shelter until it dispersed in the night. He could help a little with that. Carefully he placed himself ahead of them and with one powerful thrust of his wings he sent the smoke in the opposite direction so they could see and reach the cave his eyes had already spotted.

He rose high into the air and manoeuvred around, slowly settling on the ground to watch their progress. Good, they had found a cave. One young human girl was standing next to the river and not running with the others; what was she doing? She was looking in his direction, had she spotted him? The smoke would overwhelm her in moments. He had to decide quickly.

Staring directly at her, he widened his eyes. She saw them, screamed and ran towards the cave. He couldn't help but chuckle. Humans. This was the first one he'd seen in thousands of years. Despite everything, he felt an overwhelming sense of duty and desire to help these silly creatures. Even now, thousands of years on, their young needed help to keep them alive. They were all safely in the cave now and Pathanclaw decided to wait outside to make sure nothing befell them overnight.

He used the time to ponder about the fifth member of this little group. Who were they? Why could he not detect what they were? What were they all doing on this planet – alone with no adult humans? It couldn't be a coincidence that they were all here at the same time. Strong magic was involved. This gave him hope. If the old ways were still in use on Arcus it could make his quest easier. His great friend must still be alive, and he had sent the one to save them, as they had agreed all that time ago. Humans' lives were just a blink of an eye compared to dragons, but then his friend had a natural talent for magic. He had found a way. For the first time he felt hope in his plan. But why had he sent so many and not just the one?

While he waited, he spotted movement inside the cave. A human boy was squinting, trying to look though the smog, and there was something Pathanclaw hadn't noticed before. He trained his eyes on the mouth of a cave. He thought his old eyes deceived him, but no. Staring out into the smoke-filled air was a small dragon, but not like them. Not a youngling... he knew what it was, even as his mind tried to reject it. A magic dragon that should not be, a dragon, made, not born. What had the humans been doing now?

As the dawn drew closer, the air started to clear. Soon the humans would venture out. They had been in there for over a day with no movement, but now he sensed them stirring.

Pathanclaw decided his grandson should be the first to speak to the humans; it would be good training for him. He also needed to think and discuss this new twist in the tale, a magic dragon. He'd thought it might also be better for them to meet a young dragon first as humans had a natural fear of extremely large dragons. Actually, anything larger than them could pose a threat. But if they were used to a dragon, then maybe that wouldn't matter. After checking the humans would be okay, he took flight to go and collect his grandson. The day ahead would be the most interesting for thousands of years.

Day Two – Friendship

Triana ran through the water heedless of the cold. She quickly caught up with the others and raced ahead to the mouth of the cave, even the steep climb not eliciting a moan. As she passed them, she shouted, "There's a monster back there. I'm not lying. Everybody. Run."

The panic in her voice, rather than the command, made them all up their pace. Villian held up the phial as they made their way through the cave. They had no idea how far back it went or if they would be safe, but it was better than being out there. Thanan doubted Triana had seen a monster – she was clearly seeing things and using it as a distraction because they had left her behind.

As they all made their way inside, Villian shouted for the others to follow Thanan and he put the phial in his pocket. The heat had gone from his touch and the light went out. He retraced his steps slowly back to the mouth of the cave. The smoke was thankfully not coming in too far. He stared into the smoky air, squinting. Could he see anything? Was there truth in what Triana had said. Maybe there was something in the distance, or maybe it was the glow of this lava. He could see nothing. Feeling they were safe, at least for now, he took out the phial and followed the others. As he turned, the girl's dragon was hovering close. It looked him in the eye and twisted its head to the side before flying silently into the cave.

The cave had a moistness in the air, meaning there was probably water ahead. The deeper they went, the cleaner the air became. When they had gone far enough, they each found a rock to perch on and bent over coughing, trying to catch their breath. All except Pol, who hadn't broken a sweat. Star handed out water to everyone and they gratefully swallowed large gulps of clean, fresh water.

Villian looked at Pol. What was she? They. The terms the others used for Pol confused him. Too much was happening to focus on all the events that had developed since he'd beaten the odds and arrived here. He needed a moment to process everything and decide what to do. All these children here, their talk of magic, and dragons! Pol's strange powers. A magical dragon, if Triana could be believed. His mind was racing, even as his body acknowledged his fatigue. They all looked filthy and exhausted, they all needed to rest.

He let his battle training take over. Minimise distractions and focus on the issue in hand. They were relatively safe in the cave and away from the smoke. They all needed food and rest now until it was safe to go outside.

"Thanan, let's go further into the cave and see if it's suitable for us to sleep in tonight."

Thanan followed Villian and as soon as they moved into a side corridor the others were plunged into darkness.

Triana screamed.

Thanan rushed back, "Triana, there is no need to scream. Dragon's breath, you're going to get us all killed behaving like that!"

"It's not my fault! You left us in the dark and I was afraid those monsters were going to get us! I hate this place and I want to go home right now! Use that thing on your arm and send me home. Or else."

"Or else what, Triana?" Star had squared up to her. "Or else you will scream until the monsters come. I will tell you this now, I will push you right in their path and hope they eat you alive."

Thanan froze, he thought he'd kept the tattoo covered! Triana had seen it and seemingly knew what it was. How could she know that?

Villian made his way back and stood behind Thanan, smirking despite the seriousness of their situation. These children needed to start taking this all more seriously. He could understand why they disliked Triana but looking at her face she did look genuinely scared. He took a step forward to defuse the situation when Pol spoke. Villian noted that this sharer of secrets had mentioned something on Thanan's arm. Could it be the same as his? It had to be. This meeting was no coincidence.

"I saw the monster, too," Pol said.

Thanan decided he liked it better when Pol couldn't speak. Ever since they'd found their voice, every word had been a statement of doom. Pol looked directly at him as if they could read his thoughts. His cheeks coloured but Pol smiled, his friend wouldn't read his thoughts without his permission, if Pol could still even do that on this planet.

"Ha, told you I saw something!" Triana stomped her foot and folded her arms.

Villian ignored Triana and went to stand in front of Pol.

"What did you see, Pol?"

"Eyes."

Star shuddered. She would have put Triana's declarations down to an overactive imagination and her general air of being dramatic and wanting to be the centre of attention, but Pol, never.

Villian looked towards the entrance. He hadn't seen anything other than blackness, certainly no eyes. He was inclined to believe this strange human, but there wasn't a whole lot they could do if there was a creature out there. Looking around, he confirmed what he already knew – none of the others were armed.

"Right, we don't know what is out there. But what we do know is that we cannot go outside until the air clears. I suggest we go deeper into the cave and wait until morning. We need to rest for the day ahead. Star, Thanan, do you have weapons?"

They both shook their heads.

"Star has her big mouth," Triana couldn't help but add.

"Enough, Triana. If we are going to survive, we must work as a team. No more whingeing, no more screaming. You will do as I say, or I will leave you to face the dangers and your monsters alone," Villian said.

Thanan raised his eyebrows at this. Judging by Triana's face someone might just have managed to put the bully in her place. He risked a look at Star, who was standing, arms folded, looking very smug. That was until Villian turned his gaze on her, "I can count on you, Star? We need to work as one. Maybe Dragon could watch the mouth of the cave and alert us to any danger?"

Clever, thought Thanan. There was no point challenging Star; stubborn as they came that one. This Villian knew how to manage people and surprisingly girls. He had adapted very quickly to having them turn up at the start of this quest he was on. Thanan was sure if a magical dragon had turned up in front of him, he wouldn't have been so calm and ordered.

Star nodded and looked determined, which worried Thanan a little bit. She spoke to Dragon who flew off to settle a few feet from the entrance to the cave, ready to warn them of any perils.

"Right." Villian delved into one of the pockets on his belt and handed a rather large dagger to Thanan.

Star stepped forward and held out her hand. "I think I'd better have that one. I'm a little bit more aggressive than Thanan."

Villian looked surprised but Thanan grinned sheepishly and nodded. He would take Star over himself in a fight any day. Villian smiled and handed Thanan and Triana small daggers.

"They are all I have got, but they may be some use if we have to fight."

Thanan doubted it, none of them had ever fought with weapons in their life. It was the first time he'd ever held a dagger, as Villian had called it. It felt very heavy and unnatural to him.

He held out one to Pol, but they shook their head. He'd been hesitant even to offer Pol one. More and more Pol seemed like a part of the surroundings, part of the... he couldn't think what the word was. But even to a Prince, a warrior born, it didn't seem right for Pol to hold a weapon.

They moved deeper into the cave and found a spot which wasn't perfect but would have to do. It was cold and they huddled together, covered by their blankets. Villian offered to do the first watch, even though Star's dragon was covering the entrance. He felt better knowing one of them was awake and watchful. He also needed to come up with a plan and wouldn't sleep until he had one.

Hours later Thanan took over the watch and Villian joined the jumble of bodies on the floor. How easily they had become a pack. His initial wariness of this strange group had worn off quickly. They had been together such a short time, but had already been through so much. Tomorrow he hoped the smoke would have cleared and then he would be able to get his quest back on track. His must continue to find a dragon and save his world. Right now, he felt further than ever away from this goal, but looking at Star's strange dragon, it gave him hope that they did still exist.

Day Three – Information

Despite everything, they all slept well. Pol had taken over from Thanan and not woken anyone else until the morning of the following day.

Villian was the first to wake. He looked at the people who had become his new companions. Triana was slightly apart from the group. From the little they'd said they hadn't been friends in their world. He could see why, even after this short time. Triana wasn't a likeable kind of person. But equally this rift could be useful to him. One of the few things his father had taught him were to exploit people's relationships. Star's long legs were sticking out of the end of her blanket. Villian smiled, he couldn't help but like her. She was feisty and reminded him of his betrothed; Lady Cartina. He wondered how she was fairing as he fiddled with the ring she'd given him. With his disappearance would something happen to her? Cartina was so gentle but Star was tall and solidly built and that long bright blue hair was a statement if ever he saw one. Moving onto Thanan, perhaps the leader of this pack, his face looked wise beyond his years. What kind of world had they come from?

Thanan had said that at thirteen the children were removed from his world. Villian didn't know why that would be. The mention of Masters had been interesting; they must be the same as Raykan had spoken of, and the ones that threatened Arcus. It couldn't be coincidence that they had arrived on this planet at the same time. It must mean something. Then there was the magical dragon and the marking on Thanan's arm – was it the same as his? Today he would get more answers, because he needed to see how these new companions could help him achieve his goal.

Carefully he made his way past the others and joined Pol looking out to the entrance of the cave. Light was streaming in and the smoke had disappeared. Pol didn't look at him. He decided it was time to try and glean some more information from this strange creature, for his mind couldn't believe she was truly human. So much was strange about this place.

He perched on the edge of one of the rocks. Pol looked up and smiled at him, the strange purple eyes assessed him. He felt naked beneath their gaze. It threw him off balance and he couldn't think what to say.

Pol's mouth curled slightly, "You've slept a long time. It's another day."

Villian was shocked to hear they had slept the whole day away, although he felt better for it, if a little stiff. Since arriving here, there had been no proper time to rest and his bruises were still hurting from the fight back on Arcus.

He stretched his legs and sighed. "Did you get any sleep?"

Pol shook their head.

Somehow, he got the feeling Pol didn't need it. What was she? Or they, as the others named them.

"Can you tell me about the place you came from, Pol?"

Pol was silent for a few moments. Villian studied their face and realised that the eyes staring back at him were now orange and with shock he realised that this girl was now a boy. The changes were subtle but startling. What magic was this? He'd never heard of such a thing, even from Raykan. Villian marvelled at the world he was only just discovering; ever since Raykan had shown him that magic really existed, stranger and stranger things were happening.

Pol shook their head.

He'd thought he'd heard one of the others say this Pol was a person or creature of few words.

"I will speak to the others later. But it would be useful to know who you all are and what your plans are. Where are you all going?"

He was met by silence. Villian felt frustrated. He was hoping he could obtain more information out of them if he spoke to them individually. Divide and conquer, his father would say. Maybe Triana would be the one to speak to, she didn't seem to care what she said. They were a funny group. He decided to change his questioning.

"Can you tell me more about the monster? What did you see?"

"Big eyes."

Villian inwardly sighed. He guessed that 'big' was an improvement on just eyes from the other night. He tried again.

"What colour were they?"

"Red."

This was going to be a long conversation.

"Do you know what it was?"

Pol shrugged.

Villian decided he'd chosen the wrong one out of the group to speak to. He clearly wasn't going to get anything from Pol. He wondered if he should try a different approach. He purposely hardened his voice.

"Look, Pol, we are all here together and if there are monsters out there then we are all in danger, including your friends. I suggest you try and be a bit more helpful."

They were not afraid of him, he could see that, neither were they shy. Pol looked directly into his eyes. Villian felt he could get lost in their eyes. Something flickered and in his mind's eye he could see strange worlds and flocks of dragons. Pol smiled at him.

"Leave Pol alone Villian. If you need to know anything then I will tell you."

Villian felt shocked by the vision and Thanan's appearance. He hadn't heard him coming, which was either a testament to his skills or because Pol was distracting him. There was a lot more to this group than met the eye. He needed to stay alert. He could still face dangers; he couldn't let his guard down so easily and he realised that he had armed this little band – maybe that was a mistake.

Thanan perched next to Pol and put his arm around them. Pol leaned their head onto his shoulder and closed their eyes, looking instantly relaxed.

"Pol doesn't really like talking to other people, especially people they don't know."

"Yes, I became aware of that very quickly."

Thanan smirked at him, and Villian was sure he could see a flicker of a smile from Pol.

Villian reached inside his rucksack and handed Thanan some meat and then the skein of water. He found people opened up when they had a full belly.

"What a night. Do you think they truly did see a monster?" Villian asked Thanan.

"Pol said so and doesn't lie. If it had just been Triana then I would have doubted it."

"What is it with you two?"

Thanan sighed. He knew it was time to talk and not just about Triana. He decided to just get it over with. "Our world is called Luminosa. Children appear but we cannot remember our lives from before; well, maybe some glimpses. Once we turn thirteen, we disappear and never return. No-one knows where the children go."

Villian let that settle in. Despite his father's coolness towards him, at least he had a stable home and a purpose. He couldn't imagine what kind of life these children had already had.

Thanan wanted to trust Villian, but would it put him and his friends at a disadvantage if he told him everything? Then again, what did they have to lose? From what he'd seen, they needed each other.

"Luminosa is a strange planet. Different to here. The sky is constantly changing colour. I've only seen it blue and then black here. When children arrive, they are tested to check for their, erm, abilities. The Masters don't have that much to do with us. We are all kept in a camp most of the time."

"A camp, as in prisoners?"

"Yes, I guess you could say that. It's how it feels to us. Especially the ones the Masters don't like. Some of them, like Triana, seem to get away with more than others."

Villian added that to the list of things he knew about Triana, and it didn't paint a pretty picture about her character. He could fully understand why they didn't want her here. Why had she come with them? They said it was by accident, but was it?

"What about Arcus, do you have Masters there?" Thanan asked, keen to glean as much information as he was giving away.

Villian recognised the ploy and acknowledged Thanan's negotiating skills.

"I think it's time for us to be honest. It's clear to me there are many similarities to our situations. I don't think we have met by chance. I promise to be truthful if you will do the same."

Villian held out his hand to this young boy whom he already respected.

Thanan was shocked and impressed by Villian's directness. Perhaps he really was a prince. Thanan had never met a prince before. He'd heard stories from other children about kings and queens but had never thought to meet anyone like this in his lifetime. Then again, when all you know is that everyone disappears and probably dies at thirteen you try not to hope for too much.

Thanan shook Villian's hand. A pact had been made.

"I am happy to go first," Villian said, "to prove my words are my bond."

"As I told you yesterday, I'm on a quest. Arcus is under attack by possibly the same Masters you face, but we do not yet know the size of the force. We know their armies are building, but we do not know who commands them. We have made strong allegiances with other families."

Thanan interrupted, "So you're saying the Masters on our world are the same ones on yours? How can that be? How can they travel without the portal being open?"

"I don't know, Thanan. For many thousands of years dragons and humans lived side by side in friendship on Arcus. The presence of the dragons meant there was only ever petty fighting. But sadly, one of the Masters tricked one of the dragons into sharing their magic powers. There was a terrible battle but eventually the dragons had to leave to survive. The Masters had created something that meant we could no longer live in unison. We were making the dragons sick. Despite our powerful allies there were other forces at work."

Villian explained about the battle at the end when he left Arcus, when Raykan and his friends helped him to pass through the portal. He couldn't hide his emotion from the telling. He didn't know how his friends had faired; but he feared the worst.

"So, your friend Raykan could do Magic then? Can you?" Thanan asked, shocked to hear that there were worlds where people could perform magic without control or guidance.

"Sadly, the knowledge of magic came too late for me to learn. Raykan only taught me the very basics. He said the rest would come in time and I had to be patient. I'm afraid that Princes are not known for this virtue."

Thanan smiled, "We could perform magic back on Luminosa. The abilities I spoke of..."

It was Villian's turn to nod, he'd suspected as much. Star had said as much in their first encounter. But sometimes it was best not to force a confession.

"...When a child arrives on the planet, as I said, they are tested. Some, like Star go on to grow and train a creature. Triana and I were trained in the art of magic spells."

"But you cannot do them here?"

"No, our powers simply won't work here. We've tried."

"How does Star still control Dragon then? Surely that is 'magic'. Why hasn't her dragon disappeared?"

"I don't know. Even though we have these powers, we were never told much about them, where they come from or how they work. I've been thinking about this and I wonder if it's because Dragon was sort of 'made' by Star. Maybe they are linked so strongly that they no longer need magic to work? Although saying it out loud, it sounds a little stupid."

"Not at all Thanan. I know less than you about magic, but I can see that it could be true. Star has an extraordinarily strong bond with Dragon. Maybe they are working together, like a symbiosis."

Thanan didn't know what that was and didn't want to ask, so he just nodded.

"Dragon seems to have already grown in the last couple of days."

"Maybe the trip through the portal has boosted the magic they already had inside them? Also, Star is a child and despite her size, she is still growing so why not her Dragon?"

Thanan looked a little annoyed and Villian hastily added, "Sorry that sounded rude. I'm used to children of your age being just that. On my world they are allowed to be children, well unless you're a prince of course and then you're born an adult."

Thanan smiled. The more they talked, the more they had in common.

"Well, if we come up with enough ideas, one of them will be true and then we might discover a safe path."

They chuckled softly together; their bond strengthening.

"How does it feel when you use magic? And who trains you – is it the Masters?"

"It difficult to explain, when you do complex spells it feels like a thrumming through your body. It's difficult to concentrate and build the magic to the point where you release it."

Villian looked confused.

"Sorry, I'm not explaining this very well. Tobias would be ashamed of me."

"Tobias?"

"He was my trainer, and my friend. He helped us escape. Taught me the spells to get us through the portal and leave safely."

"Why did Tobias not come with you?"

"Ha – I would love to have seen that!" Triana's voice spoke behind them.

Thanan sighed and Villian shot her a look of annoyance which made the smirk die on her lips. He understood more and more why they disliked this girl. He decided this conversation would have to continue at another time. His instinct was telling him that the less this girl knew the better.

Triana continued but was clearly mindful of the look. "Has Thanan not told you what the trainers look like?" Thanan was about to interrupt, not because he didn't want Villian to know, but he wanted to be the one to talk to Villian, to be useful to him and treated as an equal. Yet again, Triana was spoiling everything.

"They are massive worms! Basically, we go into a cave and get chosen by a worm. I was chosen by one of the best ones." After a look from Thanan she added, "Well, obviously Thanan got the old, wise, all-knowing annoying Tobias. But I got one of the top trainers who is coveted by all the other children. Who wants an ancient, grumpy worm anyway?"

"Worm?" Villian questioned.

"If you've finished, Triana!" Thanan turned to look at Villian, "Our trainers live in a cave inside a mountain. They have been there since the worlds began – or so we are told. They know everything and train the children in different magical abilities and teach us about other worlds."

"Thanan just happened to be chosen by the best worm in existence." Star had now joined them in conversation. "The great worm Tobias. Excuse Triana. She is just jealous that no-one had probably ever been picked before Thanan."

The pride in Star's voice made Thanan look down, whilst Villian looked at Thanan with a new respect. Worms – he would need to speak to Thanan more on this subject. In all his learning he'd never heard about giant worms.

"I'm starving, what are we breaking the fast with?" Star said, stretching her long limbs and making her knuckles crack.

Thanan smiled. He was glad Star was with him.

"Do you think we could risk going outside?" Thanan asked Villian.

"I will check."

Villian made his way cautiously to the entrance. He'd drawn his sword, mindful that there had been talk of monsters.

The day was bright outside. The sun beating down from high above; suggesting it was already midday. They had slept a long time. The smoke of last night had gone, but ash covered the ground. He wondered again about the monster Triana and Pol had seen. He couldn't see anything, just the flowing river and beyond that, the flat plains into the distance and more mountains.

They all smelt of soot and the river looked inviting. Villian called to the others that it was clear, and he made his way out of the cave and over to drink from the clear fresh water. After quenching his thirst, he splashed it over his face, shaking his long hair free – it felt good and the slight wind caught it, delivering a welcome breeze on his neck. When he looked up a dragon the size of a house was glaring at him.

Day Three – First encounters

Before leaving, Pathanclaw had prepared his grandson about the ways of humans and what he should do not to appear threatening. Under no circumstances was he to use fire, raise his voice or rise to his full height. He should remain calm and seem as small as possible until the humans got used to him. Pathandon nodded throughout, taking his first important task seemingly in his stride. Pathanclaw hoped he would remember everything. He could already feel the excitement building in his grandson that he was going to meet humans for the first time. If he accidentally burnt them to a crisp it would not be a good start.

Pathandon had healed well and his wing was no longer a problem. The magic had already increased his size. Pathanclaw could tell he would need more time to train his grandson properly on how to the use the magic. It came naturally to dragons, but there were still the words that were needed for the most complex spells. They had taught the younglings on Suntra sooner than was normal practice, knowing that at some point they would need to defend themselves or others. But a spell cast incorrectly could be devastating.

After they had given the human children a full day to recover, Pathanclaw had heard a stirring inside and decided it was time. He would have liked to have given them longer, but he was eager to see if these humans were a result of his old friend or if they would need to look elsewhere. The Festival of Time portals were open to many, although he was sure many worlds had lost the power to move through them and he felt the urgency to get back to his family.

As the sun passed the middle of the day, Pathandon followed his grandfather. They circled for a while before Pathanclaw settled on the mountain above as his grandson landed adjacent to the cave and on the other side of the meandering river. Pathanclaw had said it would make the humans feel safer to have something between them. Pathandon hadn't bothered to protest. Were humans so stupid that they didn't think he could burn them to a crisp from a far greater distance? Why could a mere river offer protection? But he bowed to his grandfather's knowledge.

He waited.

Villian raised his sword knowing it would be useless against this mighty creature. Inside his emotions flickered from fear, to hope and back again. Standing right in front of him was the object of his quest. His vindication for his so-called childish belief. In seconds, he imagined the expressions on the faces of his father and the council when he returned on a dragon! That was, if it didn't eat him right now or burn him to dust and put an end to his hope and glory.

They eyed each other; dragon – human. The first meeting in thousands of years.

Pathandon wondered what all the fuss was about, this tiny creature that he could burn in seconds, even with his limited fire. He could pick it up and crush it with the talon that was a third of the size of his grandfathers'. Why? Why had his grandfather decided to save these insignificant creatures? But he'd been taught better. Through stories and lessons, he'd learned to have respect for these humans. Once they had lived in peace and it had been his mother and father's hope, his grandfather's wish, and he would see it done.

Villian marvelled at the red dragon. The sunlight reflected off its scales. The large deadly talons were as scary as the huge mouth, which gleamed with sharp white teeth, which looked as if they had blood on them, but he decided not to focus on that. If this was going to be his last moment on earth he wanted to take in every detail. He wasn't prepared for the size of this majestic creature. He now understood why his father's throne room was so big, as though it could encompass something far larger than the dragon before him. Surely, they couldn't be bigger than this?

Finally, the dragon spoke, much to Villian's shock.

"I am Pathandon, grandson of King Pathanclaw. It is an honour to meet you Prince Villian, future King of Arcus."

The sound was strange to Villian's ears. Was it talking or was he just hearing it in his mind? Thanan had said that Pol and Star could communicate this way on Luminosa but had been unable to do so here. Its mouth didn't seem to move. He struggled to comprehend how it could be so. This dragon knew who he was! Had it been listening?

Pathandon wondered what to do next. Maybe this human was a bit stupid, a bit like his friend Bluewing? All action and no intelligence? He stopped himself from talking to his grandfather. He had to deal with this on his own. He tried again, "Can you speak?"

Villian realised he'd been staring at the dragon and some moments had passed since it had asked its question. Some Prince he was.

He grabbed hold of his status and training and stood up straight. Realising that his sword was completely useless he sheathed it and eyeing the dragon said, "I am Prince Villian Palell of Arcus, my father is King Palell and ruler of Arcus. I'm here to take you back to Arcus and join our..." Villian stumbled slightly on the words and cursed himself, "...great species once again."

Inwardly he sighed. Some first speech. Species! Join? This dragon could use him as a toothpick!

So, he was from Arcus! The world his kin had fled from. The place they were trying to return to help them. It was true then. The humans were in danger and needed rescuing. He felt the relief of his grandfather. His great friend had not died in vain. Although Pathandon didn't know if the death of a great warrior like Battlewing was worth saving this human, this Prince, he was sure that Bluewing would agree.

His speech had clearly not impressed this mighty dragon. Before Villain could reply in a more dignified manner, he heard a noise behind him. Out into the daylight emerged Thanan, Star and Triana, daggers held high, screaming in a way they obviously thought was scary but sounded like three children playing pretend battles back on Arcus.

Villian shook his head. Dragons help them. He turned, expecting to see the bright red light of flame emerging from the dragon, burning them all to a crisp before his quest had been completed. Instead the dragon appeared to be laughing.

Day Three – Allegiances

His rescuers stopped in their tracks at the sound of the dragon laughing. It wasn't what they had expected when they'd decided to charge out and help Villian, Star and Thanan had been surprised that Triana had agreed to join them. Only Pol stayed back; but then, they didn't have a weapon.

Thanan looked at the dagger in his hand, and the dragon in front and despite his fear, started laughing. Admittedly, it started off with a bit of hysteria but when the others joined in they soon had tears streaming down their faces.

Through the laughter, Star said, "Might as well burn to death laughing." And that set them off again. Finally, Villian made a motion for them to all calm down. The dragon so far hadn't burnt them to death and was looking at them as if he maybe regretted this decision. Maybe it had been laughing because it was going to now burn them all to ash that covered everything around them.

Barring a few hiccups from Star, they all calmed down and moved closer to Villian, their eyes never leaving the dragon. Just as Villian was about to speak he saw a flash of something pass him. Next minute Dragon had settled in front of them; her wings fanned out – but even though she had grown, Dragon was still only slightly bigger than a small dog. She was making a god-awful noise and blowing intermittent puffs of smoke and flame in the direction of the bemused dragon. It moved forward slightly to look at Star's creature and Triana yelped a little bit.

The dragon stepped back.

“Dragon, get back here now.” Star hissed, “Sorry about that, erm, massive scary red dragon, Dragon is very protective of me. She didn’t mean to, erm, challenge you.” Star grabbed Dragon, and with difficulty, pulled her back.

“It is good to see that you have a protector. If we’d known you had a ferocious dragon on your side, then we would have not come here to help you.”

Pathandon realised his mistake by saying ‘we’. He could see the one called Prince Villian had registered his mistake. Most of them were staring back with mouths agog. Had they never heard a dragon speak before? But he supposed not. The humans were dressed very differently. One thing his grandfather had impressed on him was to take in details about humans. They’d been told about clothes they used to cover their skins. Another strange trait of a human. Prince Villian was dressed vastly differently from the others and his dark features were striking and commanding. The others had been discoloured from the sun, especially the one called Star, whose hair reminded him of Bluewing.

Villian cleared his throat and stepped forward, slightly away from the others. Clearly this dragon didn’t mean them any immediate harm, or else he was sure they wouldn’t be still breathing. If he was going to fulfil his promise to Raykan, he needed dragons, and Pathandon had said they were there to help. He’d said his grandfather was the King, did that mean this dragon was a prince, like him? No matter, he needed dragons and he had to learn to command them to return with him.

Before he could speak, the dragon spoke again, “Prince Villian it is nice to meet you, and your companions.” Pathandon hoped he was saying the words correctly. He’d been taught how to address royalty. He understood that this small human would one day rule Arcus, but Pathandon still couldn’t work out why dragons protected humans with their lives. They were so small; what did they have to offer a dragon?

Villian nodded, unsure what he expected from his first meeting with a real dragon. It wasn't this.

"I'm honoured to meet you, great dragon." Villian bowed, an honour usually only reserved for the King. "Do I address you as Pathandon or do you have a more formal name?"

Behind him, he heard Star snigger at his tone of speech. Already he knew she would tease him about it later. He realised this pleased him.

"How redress of me. Yes, please call me Pathandon, son of Pathandon, grandson of great King Pathanclaw, the mighty leader and ruler of all dragons; the King of Suntra and ruler of Arcus; along with your King of course," Pathandon hastily added, bowing his head and hoping he'd said everything correctly. He could feel the judgement of his grandfather.

Villian had never heard of Suntra before. Was this where the dragons had been expelled to when they left Arcus? Pathanclaw was the name Raykan had spoken. It had to be the same dragon, and this was the grandson of the great dragons of old.

"It is an honour to meet you, Pathandon. May I introduce my friends?"

"That will not be necessary, I know who you all are."

Villian tried not to look shocked. So, they had been listening to them in the cave. He went through everything that had been said last night and this morning. But then, did it matter what they had heard? If they were to be friends and allies in the coming war, they needed to be open with each other. As he had started to be with Thanan. He didn't want to carry on the legacy of his father, all secrets and lies.

Villian peered over and saw that Pol was not with them. He raised his eyebrows at Thanan, and he gestured to say that Pol was still in the cave and shrugged.

Thanan thought that Pol would love to see the dragon since it had affected Pol so much seeing the dragons chained up on Luminosa.

"I would like to prepare you for meeting my grandfather. After seeing your reaction to my presence, I thought it wise for you to be ready. Our discussions would be better if we were all together."

They all looked up to the sky hearing a sound like a thousand birds in flight. Dragons could be silent if they so wished, but Pathanclaw decided to give them a few moments to get used to his size. Also, he didn't get the chance to show off very often. This was an important moment for him. Here, on this planet, was the protector of Arcus, the very humans he had made this dangerous journey to protect.

Thanan gasped in awe, as the gigantic dragon swooped in from behind the mountains. The wingspan was immense. He looked at Pathandon; he'd thought this dragon was full grown! The new one, King Pathanclaw, was at least three times bigger. The sunlight glinted off the red scales, dazzling them, so they had to raise their arms to protect their eyes. He landed gracefully and without disturbing the air around him; something Thanan wouldn't have believed if he hadn't witnessed it.

The new dragon turned to Villian. "Prince Villian. It is an honour to meet you. My grandson and I are immensely proud to meet humans once again. We would like to join you on your quest and defeat your enemies, if you will have us?"

Star snorted. "Well, of course we will have you. You're dragons, big bloody dragons."

Villian turned to look at Star, who shrugged and whispered, "What? Oops sorry, am I not allowed to talk?" She put her hands over her mouth, but he could see the mirth in her eyes. Dragons save them, she was going to be a handful. His father would have locked her up for interrupting him.

"Thank you, King Pathanclaw. We are also honoured to meet you and of course I would formally," (he emphasised the formally for Star's benefit) "like to accept your help. Once again, our kingdoms will be joined. Dragons and humans will live peacefully side by side as should be the natural way."

"Once we've killed all the bad people, of course," Star whispered and grunted when Thanan nudged her in the side.

Pathanclaw looked fondly at these human children. He'd forgotten what strange creatures they were, how all of them looked the same until you got to know them, their personalities so different. He envied his grandson; this was a whole new experience for him. It was entertaining to see him interact with the humans for the first time. Children and younglings deciding the fates of the worlds. It brought him joy to see this new generation, the future hope of humans and dragons living once again. This was the start of a longer road; it would be longer than Pathanclaw had ever expected.

"I'm starving! Is it time for food now?" Star said. Villian marvelled at how quickly they had all just got used to dragons. Not moments ago, it was only a dream that these great creatures existed and now here they were pledging faith in each other and Star was once again thinking of her stomach. In response, his stomach betrayed him by groaning very loudly.

Star didn't try to hide a laugh and Villian allowed himself a smile. Today was turning out to be a good day. He still had much to discuss with Thanan about their home world of Arcus and the dragons, but he could see that was going to take a lot of time. As they set about collecting wood for a fire; Thanan went into the cave to find Pol.

Day Three – Name Day

Pol was hiding at the back of the cave, their body tight against the back of the wall.

"Pol, what's wrong? The dragons are not here to harm us. It's safe to come out. We are about to make some food. Everyone is starving, especially Star."

This raised a little turn in Pol's lips, as he'd hoped. He couldn't understand why Pol was like this. Thanan sat next to his friend and put his arm around them. Pol leaned their head on his shoulder. Pol felt like the sibling he'd never had. He'd never questioned why he'd accepted this strange creature into his life without judgement. He wasn't sure what Pol was and hadn't come up with many theories over the years but what did he know. All he knew was that Pol was his friend and it upset him when they were sad.

They sat in silence for a while until Star shouted that the food was ready. She was excited because Dragon had used his flame to light the kindling, clearly trying to impress the other dragons. Star was ecstatic.

"Come on, Pol. Shall we go and join the others and have some food? You don't need to speak to anyone. Just sit next to me. We need to keep our strength up. Also, you need to see the dragons. They really are amazing!"

Pol smiled at his excitement and got up. He held Pol's hand and they walked outside into the sunlight, but despite the sun, the air was chilly. Thanan raised his hand against the light until his eyes had adjusted. He looked at the new addition to their growing party. They were enjoying a feast, some kind of animal away and downwind from the camp. Villian had part of what Thanan thought was the same animal roasting above the fire.

"Look, Pol, I've got you these."

Star came over with a handful of herbs and freshly picked leaves, which she'd placed in a large leaf. Star took over and put her arm around Pol, while Thanan went to get some needed food from the fire. He was ravenous.

They ate in companionable silence for a while, all their gazes drawn in the direction of the dragons. Thanan noted that Triana had been unusually quiet since the dragons had turned up. He looked for her and she'd moved away from the fire, sitting on her own under a tree, eyeing the dragons with what he thought was fear.

Thanan grabbed some meat and took it over to Triana, unsure why he was doing so. She didn't deserve his kindness. He sighed; Star would laugh at him for even trying. He held out the meat to Triana and she snatched it without saying thank you.

"You can come over and join us you know. I don't know why you're sitting over here."

"I don't want to get to know any stupid dragons. Or sit with your stupid friends. I just want to go back home now."

Triana punched the ground.

Thanan was shocked by the outburst. How could anyone not want to meet dragons? Why was she suddenly so angry? Her eyes were filling up. Even though she had things better on Luminosa, why would she want to go back to that horrible place? He didn't understand her. He made to speak, but Triana interrupted him.

"Just go away, Thanan. I don't want to be friends with any of you. I just want to be left alone."

He shrugged and walked back to the others. Star was greedily chewing on some meat as Pol nibbled some leaves next to her.

"I don't know why you bother, Thanan. That girl is so annoying, and she doesn't realise she will need us if she ever wants to get back home. She hasn't got a tattoo on her arm. How does she think she is going to get back?"

Star took another bite and didn't see the look Thanan threw her. They were supposed to be keeping that a secret until the time was right. Triana had already nearly let on last night in earshot of Villian. He sighed deeply as she looked up.

"What? Hey, I've just realised it would have been my name day today. What with everything that has happened, today, we would have been parted forever." Hearing Thanan sigh she said, "Aren't you pleased I'm still alive and we are still together?"

That grin. What could he do? He stepped over, as Star stood up and they embraced. Despite her constantly getting into trouble and saying the wrong things at the wrong time, he was overwhelmed with gratitude that they had escaped Luminosa safely, and they had met up with what he hoped were new friends. He didn't know what they would have done without them.

"Happy Name Day, Star."

Day Three – Sharing stories

Pathanclaw was once again reminded why humans were so resilient and had survived for so long. Here they were, not hours after meeting dragons for the first time and they were eating around a fire and toasting their name day. His heart was light at the sight of it. Children had the ability to adjust so quickly, although he spotted the look of longing in their eyes when they thought he and Pathandon weren't looking. If his grandson knew that they were all thinking *'What would it be like to ride on their backs?'* he would be deeply offended.

Pathanclaw decided it was time to talk about their plans. They had spent long enough getting used to each other and they didn't have the luxury of time. He could see Prince Villian was as impatient as himself to get discussions under way. He was looking forward to hearing news of his old friend. But how much to disclose?

After they'd eaten, he set his plans in motion. As much as he would like his grandson to play a part in the decisions, he needed to get the other children away. He thought this planet appeared safe enough, but he didn't want them travelling alone. There was something about this child Triana that he didn't trust. They might have come from the same place, but she was very much set apart from the others. Even Prince Villian, who was from a different world was uncomfortable in her company. He would take their suspicion seriously until he spoke to the girl. This was the problem with humans; they were all so different.

Decision made, with a lot of argument and sulking, he sent Pathandon, Triana, Star and Dragon to search the area and go hunting for food. It wasn't necessary, as they could provide all that was needed but he wanted to speak with Villian and Thanan alone. He was fascinated and saddened by Star's Dragon. It was not born as they were; it had been made by magic, but it acted exactly like a dragon. He wondered at the power to create such a creature, and the fact that human children were being taught magic was more than worrying. The few humans that had been passed on this gift had caused the devastation of their worlds and species. If many more were now being taught, he thought all their futures were bleak.

Pol was another discussion all together. The others were not ready to know who was in their midst. He could hardly believe it, not sure if it could actually be true. He kept his thoughts closed off, not wanting to expose Pol, but it provided him with some hope.

Pathanclaw waited for the group to leave before meeting with the two boys. Prince Villian was used to leading: he'd been born to do it, training for his short life to become a king. Thanan had a quiet strength about him, and in him was the power to become a powerful leader; he just didn't know it yet. The compassion he had for others was as strong as Villian's. They would be a formidable pair if they were working for the same goal. He would have liked to include Star in this discussion. He'd warmed to the feisty child, her spirit was light, but he didn't want to alienate Triana further and maybe some time together might ease the girls' anger towards each other. He could only try.

The three eyed each other up. Thanan couldn't believe the size of Pathanclaw; he hadn't seen the dragons on Luminosa as Star and Pol had. If they were all like him, then they hadn't accurately described their size. Pathanclaw opened the discussion.

"After I overheard your conversation in the cave, honesty was what you sensibly decided, and I would like to add my honesty to this pact if you will have me. I cannot shake on it but hopefully my word will be enough."

Thanan stifled a smile, looked at Villian, and nodded. Thanan thought Villian would have more of an idea how to behave around the dragons. He was a prince after all. Thanan would never have thought that real dragons were capable of making jokes.

"Villian, you said that you had been sent on a quest by Raykan to return to Arcus with dragons, as Arcus is under threat."

"Yes. The danger is critical, just before I left the council was made aware of strange rumours coming from across the land. We know their armies grow greater by the day. But there is something else. I suspect that magic has returned to Arcus, bad magic, which we cannot fight. Sadly, my people have forgotten what you did for us. Thousands of years seem to have been enough to turn your stories into fairy tales."

"You humans do love your stories. In the spirit of honesty, your Raykan that you speak of was also my friend."

Villian nodded. "I thought you must be the dragon that Raykan spoke of. He only just let me into that little secret before I left." Still, a relief came over Villian knowing that he had completed the first part of his quest.

"He's still elusive in imparting his knowledge then?"

"That sounds like Tobias on Luminosa. Never could answer a direct question." Thanan blushed when he realised they were both staring at him. He felt inadequate to be part of this sharing of information with two such important people.

"It seems there are a lot of similarities in our stories and much to discuss," Villian answered kindly.

Thanan wanted to ask about this Raykan who was human and apparently thousands of years old but he bit his tongue. He would not show himself up and speak out of turn.

"Since we have shared some of our story, maybe you would be happy to tell us how you got here, Thanan."

Thanan sat up straight and told them about Luminosa. About the children, the magic, the trainers, Tobias, and the Masters. They must have had lots of questions, but they listened without interruption as he told his story. He trusted them, but still he left out the dragons on Luminosa. He would tell him in time as Pathanclaw had a right to know. But something told him that might change the course of the conversation and he wanted to hear their stories first.

They asked him a few questions after he'd finished speaking. They were both fascinated by Tobias but that was also for another day; it would not further their quest. It was clear that the Masters on Luminosa and Arcus were the same enemy.

Villian took up his story and told them about the night he'd left and the worry he had for his friends. Thanan was fascinated with Villian's life. He imagined being in charge of his life and being able to do whatever he wanted. But then Villian had no magic. Could Thanan give up magic? He missed the feeling it gave him when he was building a spell, when he released it and created something. He hoped that one day his powers would return. But Villian said Magic had ruined his world and made the dragons disappear. Could he give it up for the safety of others? Would he have a choice?

Pathanclaw followed with his story.

"When we realised that the end was near and the dragons would have to leave, we met in secret and further powers were given to a few select humans who could be trusted to continue in the shadows until the time came to reveal themselves. Now is that time."

"I wouldn't worry too much about your friends, Prince Villian. They are stronger than you think. You don't live for thousands of years without learning a few tricks. I'm sure you do not need to worry, although we agreed on honesty. Once they left that night they would have to hide because, I'm sorry to say Prince Villian, but it sounds like your father might be playing both sides of your fight. Or be receiving bad council."

Villian had suspected as much. It made sense, given that his father had let the enemy build until it was a force that they would struggle to deal with. But why? What would he gain from it? As it stood, would he lose Arcus and his kingdom? What would be worth that? The other part of Villian's brain, which he would access later, was thinking, thousands of years old? Just Raykan, or Ironhand and the Keeper – were they all ancient, all capable of magic? Ironhand had certainly known more about the book than he was letting on.

Thanan noticed that Villian was twisting a ring on his finger. He'd seemed do this when deep in thought. He wondered if it was from this Lady he was supposed to marry.

There was silence for a few moments as they all digested the shared stories. Tales of great deeds, betrayal, captivity, freedom, escape and friendship.

"We have dragons on Luminosa." Thanan didn't know where that came from. He wasn't sure it was even his turn to talk or if he should. He was going to keep it a secret, but he felt bad not being honest with his new friends after they had shared so much. He shuffled back on the rock he was perched on when Pathanclaw turned his massive head in his direction, the very movement causing a strong wind to pass over them.

"Tell me," Pathanclaw ordered.

Thanan did, for who disobeyed a dragon? A dragon king at that? He doubted even Star would do that. The last part was the hardest. He couldn't hear Pathanclaw's thoughts, but if a dragon could look devastated this was what Thanan saw now. He finished his story, and the silence was almost painful. Had he said too much? Not used the right words? Would the other children on Luminosa be in danger now?

Finally, Pathanclaw spoke, "I must think on this. After meeting Prince Villian I thought our path was clear. To return to Arcus and help save them, but this changes everything. Long have we wondered, hoped, that the female dragons were somewhere and we would be reunited one day."

Thanan wanted to ask how you could tell the difference. He'd not seen them himself but from Pol and Star's description they looked the same as these dragons; only maybe thinner, smaller perhaps, but they had said they were chained up and not looked after.

"But we need you to come to Arcus," Villian sounded desperate for the first time, worried about his people. "I don't know how long my city will last. My people need help now. I'm sorry about the other dragons, King Pathanclaw, I truly am. And I know we need all your kin if we are to prevail, but..."

Pathanclaw silenced him with a look, his voice soft when he answered, "I understand, Prince Villian, and it is also my quest to see Arcus safe and my family back where we should be. But we cannot abandon our kin on Luminosa, chained and abused by the Masters. There are also the children, who are being taught magic which should not be. They are being held captive. Where are they going when they turn thirteen? We cannot leave them to this life, Prince Villian. As a Prince with power and privilege it is not just your role to look after your own. A great King looks after all."

A moment later he added, "I'm sorry if my words sound harsh. You are still a young boy and have much to learn."

Villian put his hand up, about to protest, but Pathanclaw continued, "You are the most impressive human I've met from Arcus, and that includes the adults. One day, Prince Villian, you will be the greatest ruler of our worlds, of that, I have no doubt. But for now, as we all do, sometimes we need to step back and learn, to think and plan before we move forward on a path from which we cannot turn back. We must listen to others before we decide a course of action, we are unable to reverse. I will not decide alone. I promise this decision will be made by us all."

This calmed Villian down and he nodded. Thanan looked from one to the other wondering what they were going to do next and desperate to ask.

Pathanclaw looked to Thanan, "You would like to say something, Thanan? Go ahead, you're amongst friends and equal in this group."

"I wanted to ask how we are even going to travel to Suntra or for that matter, Arcus? The Festival of Time has passed. Tobias said I could use this to travel, but I don't really know how. How will we travel through time and to other worlds?"

There was silence from Pathanclaw and Villian as he pulled up his sleeve to show them his tattoo. He was still shocked that it was there. Before he could say more, Villian unclasped a leather covering on his lower arm. His matching tattoo glinted in the sunshine.

"You've got one, too!" Thanan exclaimed, marvelling again at the colours that almost seemed to be moving across Villian's arm, as if they were snakes.

Pathanclaw spoke. "This is a worrying development. This magic was passed onto only a few trusted people and should not be known across worlds. How is it that both of you have one and from different worlds? This is not a coincidence. The threat we face is more powerful than I thought. This will require more time. I need to think about what this means to us all."

"How do you move through the portal, King Pathanclaw? If you don't mind me asking of course," Thanan added in a rush, worried that he was going to be left with many questions unanswered.

The great dragon was lost in thought. But he didn't ignore Thanan's request for information. With both boys hanging on every word, Pathanclaw explained that dragons had the ability to move through worlds and time because they made the portals, and magic was a part of dragons like no other creature. They could only move through time and to different worlds during the Festival of Time, when all the portals were open and it was safe to travel.

"I didn't tell Pathandon this, or the others, but our next move to Arcus would have been difficult if you'd not made it here. Raykan and I had agreed that when the Festival of Time came again, if they needed us, we would try and return in the hope that whatever made us leave had disappeared with the test of time. It was foretold in stories passed down through time that 'the one' would arrive who could return peace and bring humans and dragons back together."

"And that person is Villian, sorry, Prince Villian," Thanan said blushing at his outburst again. He needed to learn not to let his excitement take over.

Even Villian looked a little pale. It was one thing to believe in yourself and want to do your best, it was quite another to have a Dragon King tell you that the peace of worlds rested on your shoulders. Thanan was glad it wasn't him. He felt a little sorry for Prince Villian.

Villian stretched out his hand to Thanan, "I believe brothers do not have to address each other in such a formal way, Thanan. Clearly our paths have crossed for a reason. Pathanclaw said he was expecting me, not you. Our quests lay together, and if that means we have to travel to Luminosa to rescue King Pathanclaw's kin and the other children, then this is what we must do." Villian paused before adding, "I just hope that Raykan and my friends have survived and can protect Arcus until we can return to save it."

Pathanclaw was more than impressed. His friend had chosen well. It wasn't an easy decision to sacrifice one for another when the scales of responsibility were perfectly balanced and gave you no clear choice. He was pleased. He knew the choice was a hard one, but even with himself and his grandson, if things really were that bad on Arcus, he suspected he would need all his kin to switch the balance in their favour. The question was what to do next.

"You're correct Prince Villian, and it is a hard choice, but the right one. If we left now and returned to Arcus, we would not be able to bring the peace we all desire. We need allies and plenty of them, and we cannot let innocents continue to be abused."

"The bracelets, or tattoos as you call them, are a map to your world. A key to open it. As I said, my magic can move me and others through time but it would have been unlikely that I would have survived the journey to collect my kin and return us all to Arcus to face the enemy. It was a sacrifice my wife and I were prepared to make. But your bracelets change all of that."

"How does it work then?" Thanan asked, "Oh, erm, sorry for interrupting again King Pathanclaw."

"As Villian said, we are kin now. Pathanclaw will suffice. My magic can open the portal, but your bracelets create what you might understand as a pathway, a direct route to our destination. On my own, my magic would be depleted by creating the portal as well as safe passage though. But using your bracelets will ease our passage and give us a point of direction, like a compass. We just need to decide what to do next."

"Is that all?" Thanan said, with a wry smile. Through all this serious talk Thanan was desperate to ask more about the other dragons. But this was serious talk, a bit like the war councils Villian had spoken about. Star was going to be annoyed she'd missed this.

Pathanclaw's head lifted. "The others are returning. I think it's best if we all have time to think about what to do next. It would also be better if we kept this to ourselves for now."

"I cannot keep this from Pol and Star. They are my friends and as much a part of this as anyone else. They deserve to know and have a say in what happens in their future. I cannot lie or keep truths from them. These decisions will affect them as well."

"I agree," added Villian. "We are going to need everyone we can trust. I see you omitted Triana from that."

"I wouldn't trust her as far as Pathanclaw could carry her to the stars and drop her from the sky. I feel bad in a way for keeping it from her. I wouldn't want to exclude anyone as I know what that feels like but she is not someone who can be trusted."

“I think you are wise to be cautious, Thanan. There is something about her. Tell your friends then, but far away from her hearing. I think it is time I had a talk with Triana to see why she makes me uneasy,” said Pathanclaw.

They all nodded. How strange, Thanan thought, to be discussing his future with a dragon. He made a pact with himself to ask about the other dragons the next time they spoke, and he was desperate to ask if he could ride one of them. But that seemed extremely rude – like asking Villian for a ride on his back. Thanan snorted and his cheeks felt his shame once again. His friends were gracious enough to ignore him.

He asked a question to cover his embarrassment. “Do you know where we are, Pathanclaw? Does this world have a name? From what you and others have said, this is similar to Villian’s home world of Arcus.”

“We are short of time, but simply put, this is Arcus.”

Villian gasped.

“It’s Arcus in a different time. Before humans and dragons existed or maybe even after. Maybe the future. It is difficult to tell.” Pathanclaw said the last so quietly they wondered if they’d misheard.

“Wow, so we really have gone back in time or forward in time? Star and I were talking about it and decided we must have, or else why would it be called the Festival of Time, right?”

“That is correct, Thanan. It means so much more than that, but you humans love to name an event and attach a bit of mystery.”

“Is it possible to move to different times on other worlds then?” Villian asked. In his mind he was forming a plan. Could they go back to a time before the dragons and change it?

“I know what you’re thinking, Villian, but sadly it would be against all the laws laid down for using the portals. If we went back and changed certain moments in time without need, then what is to say you were ever born. All things happen for a reason. We must recognise our limitations – not just in our powers but in our desires. If you started something like that where would it stop?"

"But what is to stop the Masters doing that?"

"I need to think on this more, Villian, and in practice, nothing, other than the fact they need more than the magic we used to travel. The Festival of Time allows us to travel here, to a safe place for the travellers to prepare to move worlds. It was created to allow dragons to escape from Arcus. It was not really meant to be used by others. The only way you can travel to the past of other planets is to gather the right forces to create this. We cannot talk about this anymore, they are coming. But it is a useful discussion for another time."

Thanan also felt frustrated. If they could go back to another time, he could go back to before the Masters took him, back to his family and somehow stop them taking him. But then with a heavy heart he realised that might mean he would never meet Star or Pol. As Pathanclaw said, it was tricky.

Thanan and Villian went to collect firewood for the camp, each lost in their own plans and thoughts, and to greet the others when they returned, hopefully with some food. Villian finally remembered the book in his backpack, he'd meant to bring this up. Pathanclaw flew off to no doubt speak with his grandson. Tomorrow they would decide what they would do next. Would they go to Luminosa first? It was going to be a long, unsettled night.

Day Four – Confessions

Pathanclaw watched Triana as she kicked a rock on the floor, making it land with a splash in the river. The others had left to go hunting and despite inviting her, she'd decided not to go along. He could hear her cursing them – he was shocked that a young female child knew such words. They'd agreed that today they would let the others know what was happening. Thanan had looked worried about telling Star.

As Pathanclaw watched the girl, he circled a few times and noticed that she was messing with something tucked inside her clothing. A glint of gold caught his eye. He focused; a talisman! She looked everywhere other than up; she turned the small object over and over in her hands before hiding it away once again.

"What?" Thanan took a step back, even though he was ready for this, the fierceness in Star's eyes made him fear for his life.

"You," she said pointing at Thanan and Villian. "Had a meeting without us?" pointing then at a frightened looking Pol and Pathandon. Pathandon didn't like to say that he knew about the meeting and his grandfather had filled him in last night. He didn't want that fury directed at him. Thanan was going to interrupt to say Pathandon wasn't there either. He looked at the dragon and gave a slight shrug in apology.

Dragon rose in the air breathing fire, which made Pol giggle despite the seriousness, their purple eyes dancing with laughter. Despite having to run around in circles to avoid

Dragon, it warmed Thanan's heart. Star glared at Pol and the laughter stopped.

By this time Star was bright red in the face, and Thanan knew she would bite his head off if he spoke right now. He'd discussed it with Villian and it was decided that Thanan would start by telling her about the meeting, they would wait until she'd 'flipped out' and then Villian would take up the story, hoping that she wouldn't take it out on Villian in the same way. Thanan saw Villian gulp and had to hide a smile. If Star saw him smile now that would be his life over. No adventure. No saving the children or dragons. Over. It amused him that even a Prince looked scared of his friend and Pathandon had taken a step back.

Once she'd finished ranting, Villian put up his hands, "Please, Star, we are sorry that you were not part of the meeting. Of course, if Triana hadn't been here, then it wouldn't have been an issue. But we needed someone to take her away so that we could talk in secret. We didn't have the time to tell you our plans. But we thank you for your part in them." Villian bowed his thanks, and Thanan could see why one day he would become a great King.

Dragon finally stopped chasing them and settled next to Star, giving the signal that she was starting to calm down. It wasn't as Villian had expected. He thought his words would instantly melt Star and have her apologising for her outburst. Instead she glared at him for what felt like an eternity. Thanan was impressed because she hadn't attacked either of them directly... yet.

Finally, she let out a long deep breath and said, "I accept your apology, Prince Villian, but please do not let it happen again. Pol does not like being left out of things, and as their friend, it is my duty to protect them."

Pol's head came up sharply at the mention of their name, clearly shocked that they were being brought into the conversation. This time Thanan had to hide the smile behind a cough. He could hear Villian struggling as well. Star really was one of a kind.

Finally forgiven but not forgotten, Villian and Thanan explained everything to Star and Pol. Pathandon nodded as if hearing the story for the first time. Thanan realised that even a great dragon feared Star. They'd thought it best for Pathandon to come with them just in case he had to carry Star off to cool down, or to protect them.

It didn't take long. Star already knew about their lives on Luminosa, so Villian had spoken more about the struggles on Arcus and Pathandon had spoken about Suntra. Villian had shown her his matching tattoo and explained how Pathanclaw had said they could use them as a compass to their worlds.

"So," Thanan said, now he felt it was safe for him to talk. "We have to decide what to do. Do we go straight to Arcus and help Villian with only two dragons?"

"Erm, excuse me!" Star said, and Dragon let out a small flame in Thanan's direction.

"Sorry, three dragons." He eyed Dragon warily.

"Do we go to Arcus and help Villian with 'three' dragons, or do we go to Suntra and collect their kin and then go to Arcus? Or do we go back to Luminosa and try and rescue the dragons and other children? Then go to Suntra and then go to Arcus?"

Star held up her hand. "Thanan, you're waffling."

"How was Pathanclaw intending to bring the other dragons through once he got here?" Star asked.

Pathandon took up the story, "As Villian said, my grandfather had formed a plan with Raykan to send 'the one' through to meet us. They could then use the bracelet to create a link for our kin to come straight through to Arcus. But we cannot just leave ours and your kin to suffer and die on Luminosa."

They were all silent for a few minutes.

"We need to rescue the dragons and the children."

Everyone stared at Pol, a person of few words was inclined to make people listen.

"Pol's right. Sorry, Prince Villian, but as much as I don't want to return to that awful world, the sight of those dragons chained up has caused me nightmares ever since. As much as I wanted to escape because I didn't want to be taken away and leave my friends, I've felt bad ever since that we didn't try and rescue them and the other children. Now we have more friends, I think we have a chance of saving them."

Pathandon was coming to realise why his grandfather loved the humans so much. They barely knew each other, and this small human child was prepared to risk her life to save his family and other children who were not in human terms, her kin. He'd found it strange that humans only considered their immediate family kin, whereas all dragons are kin.

Pathandon looked at Pol, the child had been a great part of their discussion last night as well as their plans. Pathanclaw had his suspicions about the child but wasn't ready to share them fully with him. When he'd protested, his grandfather had said that he wanted to be sure – whatever that meant.

"It is the right decision. But do we all go together, or do we split up? Do we go and collect the other dragons and then move to Suntra? From what you've said about the Masters it doesn't look like they defend the camp other than using the dragons to block the magic, and Pol is able to help with this. Do you really think we will need more dragons? How many Masters are there?"

"I've only ever seen eight, and that was when we were taken into the cave for the first time and at the gathering for the Festival of Time," Thanan answered.

"It sounds like it's not heavily guarded then, I don't see why we would have a problem." Pathandon said.

Star liked Pathandon, he was all about action. "Yeah, if we fly straight to the edge and save the other dragons, surely they will be able to help us defeat the Masters and rescue the children."

"You think your ability to create magic will return on Luminosa?" Pathandon asked. It had been a large part of their discussion last night. The fact that so many humans were being taught magic and that their powers had stopped there. He knew his grandfather was worried.

"I'm sure it will. Why wouldn't it? Star hasn't been able to communicate with Dragon the same way on this world, and although I can practice and see the spells – I cannot form them. But I think once we get back onto Luminosa, whatever is affecting us here, I'm sure it will be all right."

Pathandon looked at Pol, thinking about something his grandfather had said. Pol's eyes slowly met his.

The discussion went on for hours as they spent their time hunting. Villian had been teaching them how to track and hunt for food. Star had said it was stupid because Pathandon could just do it for them. Pol had quietly slipped off into the woods. Finally, tired and hungry they returned to the cave before it got dark. It was decided that they needed to speak as a group with Pathanclaw before the final decision was made. Whatever they did, they needed to make the right choice; the fate of Arcus and the safety of the children and dragons relied on them.

Back at the cave, Pathanclaw had slowly circled before he made his way to Triana. He gently landed on the other side of the stream and waited for her to come to him when she was ready. She looked scared, and despite his feelings and how she treated the others, he felt sorry for her. In human years she was so young, already she had also suffered more than a child should. They were not allowed to be children as in the days of old. It firmed his decision that they must go to Luminosa and save them.

After a while Triana got used to the dragon and since there was nowhere else to go, she decided to walk over and talk to him.

"Why are you not with the others?"

"Because I wanted to speak with you."

She snorted and kicked another rock, "I don't see why."

"I am sorry that you've had a terrible start to your life,

Triana. It should not have been that way. A child should be allowed to enjoy growing up, not be forced to do another's bidding."

"I wasn't forced to do anything. I liked it on Luminosa. I was learning magic and I had proper friends there and one day..."

Her voice trailed off.

"One day?" Pathanclaw questioned.

"Nothing. It's none of your business."

Triana perched on one of the large boulders but did not walk away. It was clear she was craving company, but she'd hardened her heart to survive, her exterior like a hard shell protecting her. Or maybe she was a horrible person as Star thought. Bad to the bone. But Pathanclaw knew emotions and humans were complicated. It was never as simple as being good or evil.

Pathanclaw let her settle a moment. Deciding how to respond, Triana's hand kept going to the place he knew she had hidden the amulet. He couldn't ask her about it, that would make her more secretive. This situation needed time, but it was time they didn't have.

"Maybe I can help you return home?"

Triana's head spun and she stood up. "Really, you could do that?" It was the most enthusiastic he'd seen her. So, she did want to go back then, and it was not just pretence. Maybe this was something he could use to his advantage.

"Yes, that is in my power to do. But I need you to be honest with me, Triana. I need to make sure I'm making the right decision. The others say that all the children are enslaved on Luminosa."

That snort again, "They are silly. We get taught how to do magic and get free food. We have freedom to explore and do what we like. So, what, if some of them are disciplined by the Masters, they deserve it."

Pathanclaw was sad; this child didn't realise there was a better life out there. It made him feel guilty that he hadn't acted sooner. How many more had suffered because the dragons had hidden away on Suntra too long, nursing their losses? Thinking they were saving the ones who had escaped Arcus? But had they had any choice? They'd had to wait until the worlds opened and the one arrived.

"Not all children live the way that you do. You're not free despite what you think. There is a better way, Triana. With hope..."

"Stop. I don't want to hear it and I don't care what you think. Just because you're some stupid dragon that calls himself a King. Like that stupid Prince and hangers on, Star and Thanan. I'm not interested. You can burn me alive. I don't care. I hate all of you."

With that she stormed off into the cave.

It saddened Pathanclaw's heart to see it, but he let her go. In time, maybe she would come to realise that they were not her enemy.

Day Five – Plans

On Thanan's name day they gathered in the morning light to discuss what their future plans would be. Triana had been invited and she'd typically shrugged but taken her place in the glade with them all. The day was bright and warm, and the birds were particularly vocal.

Before sitting down, Star and Pol had hugged Thanan, knowing that if they had stayed on Luminosa this would not have been their fate today. They all felt excited, yet, apprehensive about the decisions they were going to make.

Finally gathered, they shared as much as they could. The agreement was to be careful around Triana but they needed to make this decision as a group. Pathanclaw asked them to share their stories once again, this time with Star's input, which is why it took so long. She had an exhausting number of questions.

"Don't be ridiculous, there are no dragons on Luminosa. I would have seen them," Triana shouted scornfully.

Star bristled, "Why would you? You don't know everything about Luminosa. The Suckers really are dragons, Pol and I saw them. Chained up."

Pathanclaw winced as he thought of the pain his kin had suffered all these years and Pol's head dropped.

"Sorry, Pathanclaw. We wouldn't make this up. Why do you have to challenge everything, Triana? You don't know any more about Luminosa than we do."

Triana and Star were face to face at this point. Villian stood and moved them apart cautiously. "That's enough." He turned to Triana, "The things Star has said are true, Triana, and you must accept it. All, apart from you, have taken the oath to be truthful in this group. Maybe you need to start trusting us and doing the same."

Triana turned to him. Despite everything, Villian felt sorry for this girl. This child. No matter the situation on Luminosa, she, out of them all, felt comfortable and maybe even happy there. But he was mindful of the things he'd heard and seen. He saw doubt in her eyes, sadness, anger and defiance. But a child no less. She sat down again without saying anything further.

"To the matter of trust, I have something to share with you all." Villian reached into one of the hidden pockets and took out the small leather book the Keeper had given him. He untied the string that bound it and passed it around the group.

"Hey, that's the bracelets we have?" Thanan said, mindful that they were sharing more information with Triana than they had agreed, but if the plan they had discussed all morning was the path they were going to take, they couldn't keep everything a secret. He glanced at Triana, but she was pretending not to be interested, although he noticed she flicked through the book before passing it to Star. Star held it up for the dragons to look at.

"Yes. Do you know the language, Pathanclaw? Anyone?"

"For obvious reasons we do not have written language like you humans. We have a great many talents, but writing is not one of them. We haven't got the talons for it."

This elicited a smile from them all, even ever so slightly from Triana. Thanan and Star both shook their heads, unable to read it.

"Maybe it needs some kind of magical spell to uncover the words?" Thanan said. "What do you think it is for, Pathanclaw?"

"I suspect it is something that we don't want to get into the wrong hands, Thanan. I will think on it. Perhaps there is a way we can read it. You're right that it is a mystery. Magic has had a hand in making this book. I can feel it." Pathanclaw turned his head to Villian, "Did the giver of this book say any more about it?"

"No, I'm afraid not."

"It seems to me that people give us a lot of things but rarely explain what to do with them. It was the same on Luminosa. Tobias would never give me a direct answer and left many questions unanswered."

Triana looked up at this, "It was the same with my worm."

Thanan was shocked. No snide comment or threat. He didn't think he'd ever heard Triana speak like this. There was no anger, no defiance. He wasn't sure how to answer but he didn't have to worry, that's what he had Star for.

"Oh, yours was the same? I was sick of Thanan coming back day after day with nothing to tell us. What's the point of having the wisest worm ever and still knowing nothing? Waste of time. I would much rather have my Dragon."

Triana actually smiled and turned to look at Dragon. Pathanclaw noticed the longing in her eyes. Was this the real Triana they were seeing or was she pretending? Time would tell, but it was a start.

"Keep it safe then, Prince Villian, we will look at it again in time. Are we decided then?"

"Yes," Villian said, "We will stay here for three months and train. Then we will leave for Luminosa to save the children and your kin before travelling to Suntra to collect your family. We will then return to Arcus to save it from the enemy."

Those few words made the challenges they faced seem almost achievable. But they couldn't imagine the dangers and sorrow to come.

They'd decided that Villian would teach Star and Thanan as much as he could about fighting. If their magic didn't work when they arrived, they might need to rely on these new skills. Triana had declined to be involved with any of the plans despite the glimmer of interest. Pol kept silent throughout.

Thanan was overjoyed. Pathanclaw had agreed that they could learn how to ride dragons. Even Villian's jaw had dropped open when the dragon king had voiced his decision. Thanan wasn't sure if Pathandon agreed but he didn't openly object. Star had naturally said she would learn on Dragon who was doubling in size every day. Villian said she would be the size of a horse in a few days if she carried on growing that way. He then had to explain what a horse was. Villian was shocked by how little they knew. But he knew he would enjoy teaching them about Arcus, his home. It kept his quest in his mind and his thoughts, which so often strayed to his betrothed and his friends. Would the delay prove a cost they couldn't afford?

Time to leave

Three months after their thirteenth name day they were travelling back to the place they so desperately wanted to escape. But they were returning with two dragons and a Prince. Would it be enough? Would they be able to rescue the children and the dragons from the Masters' control? This seemingly impossible task achieved, could they then return to Villian's home world to save his people from their enemy?

Villian sat astride Pathanclaw, Star on Dragon, now grown to her full height. She was much smaller than the real dragons but equally impressive, her stature matched perfectly when Star sat astride. Thanan was on Pathandon's back. Pol had clapped with joy at seeing them, and quickly climbed onto Pathandon, clinging onto Thanan and laughing with delight. Their excitement was infectious and helped to lessen the anxiety they were all feeling. Triana was still sulking as she hadn't been allowed to ride and could only now sit behind Star on the back of Dragon.

Star and Thanan had naturally argued when Pathanclaw said Star had to carry Triana. Eventually, Villian had intervened, saying he needed to be free to fight, and Pol would help and not hinder Thanan. They hoped once they arrived back that their magical powers would be restored. Out of earshot of Thanan, Villian told Star that she could throw Triana off if she so much as said a wrong word. This pleased Star immensely and Thanan was shocked to see Star seemed pleased to welcome Triana onto Dragon. Triana wisely looked a little scared. Star was rarely nice to her, even though they had shown a semblance of a truce over the months.

Villian would never forget the first moment he'd climbed onto Pathanclaw. That had been a bit tricky to master, and not the same as riding a horse. It was like climbing the side of a rock-face, even when Pathanclaw had made himself as low as possible. Villian had made himself as comfortable as he could; vowing to get a leather-smith to make him some thicker clothes when he returned home. His mind had been full of ideas for creating a harness, but he wondered if these great creatures would see this as an insult. He'd not dared to bring it up yet.

That first exhilarating climb into the sky had taken his breath away. He'd clung on for dear life; he hadn't realised he'd been screaming until Pathanclaw asked him to stop. The screaming had been excitement, and not fear. It was all he'd dreamt of when he'd lain in the grass daydreaming back on his home world of Arcus. The feeling was hard to explain. Pathanclaw had gone easy on him for the first few trips letting them both get used to it. The first time for Villian, but not for Pathanclaw. He remembered the first time Raykan had ridden him. He chuckled, Raykan had been sick as soon as he'd got off.

It had been the best day of Star's life, as she knew it would be. All those years of dreaming and working. All the time she had trained day after day, hoping that one day her creature would be a dragon and that she would ride her, and they would be best friends forever. Never would she be left alone. She and Dragon were one.

The presence of the other dragons had seemed to feed Dragon even more. She'd grown big very quickly. After hearing the new dragons talk, Star was hoping that Dragon would be able to, but Dragon showed no signs so far. Star grabbed Dragon around the neck and squeezed her affectionately; it wasn't as nice as before as her feathers had given way to blue scales much to Star's delight. They matched her hair.

Pathanclaw had told her the blue dragons were the warriors and protected his family. Dragon was a protector. Star had barely slept for two days, she'd been so excited. She knew all that training had paid off – she had a battle dragon. She imagined them, fierce in combat, tracking down their enemies – burning them to a crisp in their wake.

Thanan had to have a quiet word with her and explain it wasn't nice to keep talking about tracking others down and burning them to a crisp. It was making Pol upset. More so, Thanan was sick of hearing about it, but he knew Star wouldn't shut up because of him. The mention of Pol had settled her down enough to be tolerable.

Star was happy and nervous. What would it be like? They had practised until they barely had enough strength to eat at night. Getting used to riding a dragon was harder than she had thought. It came naturally to Villian; she blushed thinking about him. She'd fallen off Dragon once in training as she was transfixed by how he looked on Pathanclaw; every bit the handsome prince. She knew he was going to marry someone on Arcus, but it all sounded a little silly to her. Making someone marry someone else. When she got married, she would decide who; she couldn't help a furtive glance at Villian who was unconsciously fiddling with his ring as he was often seen doing.

Thanan felt Pol's head on his back, trusting him to keep them safe. He, like Villian couldn't believe he was really riding a dragon. Pathandon had not been looking forward to the day when Thanan sat astride him for the first time, but after their first flight together he enjoyed the young human's excitement and it was almost like having Bluewing with him again. How strange that he already held such a strong connection with these humans, now his friends, his family.

Thanan held his arm aloft, and as the dragons chanted the magic words they rose gently into the sky. His tattoo throbbed on his arms, the colours of the bracelet swirling until they opened a portal big enough for them to enter. Their time here was at an end. It was time to rescue the dragons and free the children. Time to do battle.

Pathandon nodded and they disappeared.

Thank you for reading my novel, please do consider leaving a review on Amazon or Goodreads. Feedback helps an author to find new readers and we enjoy reading them.

Find out more about me on my website

www.clpeache.com

Other books available on Amazon.

Book Two of the Festival of Time series
will be published in spring 2022.

To any writers thinking about self-publishing, go for it, you never know where a bit of courage will take you...

Printed in Great Britain
by Amazon

62962117R00137